Tales

of

Muffled Oars

By the Same Author

The Restraint of Beasts

All Quiet on the Orient Express

The Scheme For Full Employment

Three to See the King

Explorers of the New Century

The Maintenance of Headway

A Cruel Bird Came to the Nest and Looked In

The Field of the Cloth of Gold

The Forensic Records Society

Once in a Blue Moon

Only When the Sun Shines Brightly

Screwtop Thompson and Other Tales

Tales

of

Muffled Oars

by

Magnus Mills

Published by Quoqs for Magnus Mills

Kindle Direct Publishing

2020

This book is a work of fiction. The names and characters are from

the author's imagination and any resemblance to actual persons,

living or dead is entirely coincidental.

No part of this publication may be reproduced in any form or

means without prior permission from the publisher.

Cover designed by Richard Moody

All rights reserved.

Copyright @ Magnus Mills 2020

For David Miller

1.

'England is a naturally peaceful country,' said Macaulay. 'The sporadic outbreaks of violence, conspiracy, jealousy and greed are mere interludes in a long and peaceful history. Peace, however, leaves no evidence behind. There are no scarred battlefields, no sunken ships and no ruined castles to show where peace has been. Oh, we may find a few surviving documents lying in the archives that record the time and place when peace was declared, but there remains no trace of the peace itself. Peace can be elusive; it has a tendency to slip away at the slightest disturbance, but peace is always somewhere in the background, waiting to reappear.'

Macaulay paused and glanced around him.

'Shall I continue?' he asked.

'Please do,' said Swift. 'We're all ears.'

'Our first glimpse of peace was in late spring in the year 973, when a royal barge came gliding along the River Dee. At the helm stood Edgar, King of England, and plying the oars were eight minor kings of the British Isles. A cavalcade of many boats followed behind, and according to popular memory it was a sight to behold. Yet this was no leisurely excursion up the river and back again. Rather, it was an act of submission. The visiting kings had been summoned from far and wide to pledge their allegiance to Edgar. They rowed him in state before a vast crowd of onlookers, and with each dip of the oars his supremacy was further enhanced.'

'I like that,' said Swift, 'about the dipping of the oars.'

'A very sedate picture,' added Hogarth, 'suggesting peace with dignity.'

'Viewed from a distance, maybe,' said Macaulay, 'but at close quarters the scene was far less tranquil. Those oarsmen were an unruly bunch and it took all Edgar's authority just to get them to sit next to one another in his barge.'

'Who were they exactly?'

'We don't know their names any more, but they included chieftains from Scotland, Strathclyde, Cumbria, Gwynedd, Glamorgan and the Isle of Man. You can imagine the rivalry between them. They were hardly inclined to pull together on the oars.'

'So why did they rally to Edgar's command?'

'Because he offered peace instead of turmoil,' said Macaulay. 'His byname was Edgar the Peaceable.'

'Must have taken some organization,' said Hogarth, 'getting in touch with all those kings. I mean, how did he know where they all were?'

'As a matter of fact, it was the other way round,' replied Macaulay. 'His reputation had been established for some years. They would certainly have heard about him and were doubtless keen to pay homage, which is why they all turned up on the appointed day. Needless to say, he was fully aware they had no intention of honouring their pledge. He knew they'd return home full of resentment for their English overlord and carry on much as they had before: living in dwellings with turf walls; stealing cattle from the outlying regions of his kingdom; and blaming him when their crops failed. Nevertheless, King Edgar had demonstrated what was possible. It was he who set our benchmark.'

'England at peace?'

'Precisely.'

2.

I told Gerard about my new acquaintances.

'There's three of them,' I said. 'Macaulay, Hogarth and Swift, and they all wear these tailcoats with shiny buttons up the front.'

'How did you meet them?'

'Well, I just sort of came across them really. I was actually looking for Room 412, but I must have taken a wrong turning or something. I heard voices at the end of a corridor, so I wandered up and found this open door. They were all sitting around in big comfortable armchairs with a fire blazing in the corner. Funnily enough, Macaulay gave me a nod as if they'd been expecting me, and next moment I was ensconced in a chair with a glass of port at my side. All very civilized.'

'Sounds like it.'

'Macaulay was holding forth on the subject of England at peace. It seems to be a kind of fixation with him. He insists that peace is our natural condition and always has been.'

'Really?' said Gerard. 'What about all the rebellions, riots, persecutions, plots and murders?'

'Apparently they're aberrations which obscure the underlying state of peace.'

'Ah.'

'Although peace doesn't necessarily mean tranquillity.'

'What does it mean then?'

'Well,' I said, 'Macaulay can explain it much better than I can. Why don't you come along next time?'

'Alright,' said Gerard. 'I will.'

3.

'In some countries,' said Macaulay, 'peace occurs in regular cycles. There's a straightforward explanation for this: peace brings prosperity; prosperity brings pride; pride brings confrontation; confrontation brings warfare; warfare brings desolation; desolation brings peace and so the cycle is completed.'

'Is it a proven hypothesis?' enquired Swift.

'In most cases, yes, and especially on the continent where all the countries are jammed up against one another; but for some reason the rule doesn't seem to apply here. Peace in England occurs entirely at random.'

'Like the weather,' said Hogarth.

'Quite,' said Macaulay, 'and I'm afraid to say that after King Edgar died the skies darkened for many years.' He paused again. 'The culprits, of course, were the Danes.'

'Oh yes, the Danes,' said Swift. 'I'd forgotten all about them.'

'Danes, Vikings, Norsemen. Call them what you will, but forget them at your peril.'

'I thought they'd been suppressed by Alfred the Great.'

'Suppressed, yes, but never expelled. They'd been living quietly in the north and east for more than a century, but their seafaring cousins were still on the loose and they could tell a weak king when they saw one.'

'Æthelred the Unready?'

'Correct,' said Macaulay. 'The king who believed that peace could be bought at any price. No sooner had he succeeded to the throne than seaborne attacks began on every harbour in the realm. The raiders had speedy longships, and they could easily outrun any English vessels. Æthelred's response was to pay them to keep away (Danegeld it was called), but actually it only encouraged them to come back for more. Soon every ruffian in the northern seas had heard about the Danegeld. In consequence, the raids became more frequent, penetrating ever further inland and gradually transforming into full-scale invasions. Finally, King Sweyn Forkbeard of Denmark landed on these shores, along with his son Canute. Standing against them was Edmund Ironside, the last of the English kings.'

4.

'Have you noticed,' said Gerard, 'there aren't any clocks in that room of theirs?'

'Nor any windows,' I replied. 'Yes, I've noticed.'

'It feels disconnected from the outside world.'

'Yes.'

'You can't even tell whether it's night or day.'

Gerard and I were discussing the hour or two we'd just spent with Macaulay, Hogarth and Swift.

They'd shown no surprise when I'd brought my friend along. They'd merely nodded us into the room, allowed us a few moments to settle into our armchairs, then resumed their conversation. As usual the subject was England at peace, with Macaulay taking the lead while Hogarth and Swift passed the occasional comment. At one stage, during a lull, Hogarth had risen to his feet and poured everyone a glass of port. Once he'd returned to his chair, though, he didn't move again; neither did Macaulay or Swift. They appeared content to stay just where they were, with a fire blazing in the corner and no windows or clocks to remind them of time going relentlessly by.

'For all we know,' I said, 'they might have been in that room forever.'

'Seems that way,' said Gerard. 'You certainly get the impression they never go anywhere else.'

'They don't really need to.'

'No, probably not.'

'They're totally immersed in history.'

Over the next few minutes Gerard said nothing more. I could sense he had something on his mind, and I assumed he was contemplating the various aspects of England at peace. It soon transpired, however, that his sights were set a good deal lower.

'I've been thinking,' he said at length. 'Why don't we invite the three of them to the Royal Oak?'

I peered at him in astonishment.

'Blimey,' I said. 'Never thought of that.'

'Obviously.'

'I doubt if they've ever been to a pub.'

'Well,' he said, 'they drink port, don't they? They sell several kinds in the Royal Oak so it wouldn't be a problem. Or they may even wish to sample a pint of Guinness. I'm sure they'd enjoy it. Especially Hogarth; he looks just the type you find in the public bar.'

'Yes,' I said, 'come to think of it, he does.'

'Shall we ask them then?'

'Alright, but you can do the asking.'

5.

'Peace remained hidden from view,' said Macaulay, 'until the autumn of 1016. By then both Æthelred and Sweyn Forkbeard were dead; meanwhile, Edmund Ironside and Canute had fought one another to a standstill. Eventually, a truce was proposed and the exhausted armies made camp on opposite banks of the River Severn, with the English on one side and the Danes on the other; then the two kings were rowed in fishing boats to an island midstream.'

'More boats,' remarked Swift.

'Indeed,' said Macaulay, 'but this time there was no dignified procession up the river and down again. The two kings had met to resolve the conflict, and the result was a carve-up. They agreed that Edmund Ironside would rule in the south, while Canute would have all of the north. Seemingly the dark clouds had parted, but then Edmund died within weeks of signing the treaty and the wind changed yet again. Winter was approaching, the country was laid low and the people were tired of fighting. There was no longer any choice to be had, and as the year turned Canute was proclaimed king of all England.'

The flames crackled in the hearth, but for a while all else was silent. I sat in my deep, comfortable armchair trying to imagine England in the mid-winter of 1016, with the snow falling and a Danish king newly-installed on the throne; and then my eyes began to stray. I looked at the row of pegs where Macaulay, Hogarth and Swift had hung their tailcoats with shiny buttons up the front; I saw a bottle of port on the dresser; then I found myself gazing at the wall above the fireplace, where some words had been inscribed in bold letters:

CONSIDER HISTORY, WITH THE BEGINNINGS OF IT STRETCHING DIMLY INTO THE REMOTE TIME, EMERGING DARKLY OUT OF THE MYSTERIOUS ETERNITY: THE TRUE EPIC POEM AND DIVINE UNIVERSAL SCRIPTURE.

I'd seen these words before somewhere, and vaguely I pondered who might have composed them. I had to admit they appealed to me. I quite liked the idea of Macaulay, Hogarth, Swift and myself lounging around 'considering history' in such lofty terms. (I wasn't so sure about Gerard though; there were long periods when he appeared to be paying no attention whatsoever.)

The silence continued a little longer, then finally Hogarth spoke.

'Did Canute restore the peace?'

'Yes, he did,' replied Macaulay, 'but he charged a high price for it. He'd seen for himself how easy it was to extract Danegeld from the English people, so his first act was to raise a punitive tax to cover the cost of the invasion. Over the following months he occupied London and moored his fleet at Southwark; and on feast days he personally steered the royal flagship along the Thames.'

'In homage to King Edgar,' suggested Swift.

'Possibly,' said Macaulay, 'but more likely as a demonstration of his own authority. The peace had been hard won, and Canute was desperate to keep hold of it.'

All of a sudden Gerard raised his hand, and I glanced across at him with alarm. For a moment I thought he was going to mention a trip to the pub, which would have been most inappropriate while Macaulay was in full flow. To my relief, however, he simply asked a question.

'Is this what's known as 'the king's peace'?'

Macaulay gave Gerard a penetrating look.

'Have you been reading ahead?' he enquired.

'No, no,' said Gerard. 'I just wondered, that's all.'

'Well, yes, as a matter of fact, Canute's reign is a perfect example of the king's peace. The idea was that if people accepted the king's rule, and obeyed him, they could expect to live in peace under his protection.'

'And if they didn't?'

'They were outlawed.'

'So it was take it or leave it.'

'Correct,' said Macaulay, 'and most chose the king's peace.'

6.

After our departure, I turned to Gerard and said, 'You didn't mention about going to the pub.'

'No, I didn't,' he replied. 'There wasn't a suitable opening.'

'No, I suppose there wasn't.'

'Still, there'll be plenty of opportunities in the future.'

'You're going to continue coming then?'

'Of course.'

'By the way, how did you know all that about the king's peace?'

'I remembered it from 'LOOK AND LEARN'.'

'Oh,' I said, 'I used to have that delivered.'

'And me,' said Gerard. 'When I was a child my parents made me read it instead of a comic.'

'I've still got all my copies.'

'Yes,' he said, 'thought you would have.'

'You can borrow them if you like.'

'No, thanks anyway, but it's easier to listen to Macaulay.'

7.

'Canute had two sons by two wives, and when he died the succession was disputed. Harold Harefoot was the first to grab the crown, but he only lasted five years and then he, too, was dead. Next came Hardicanute. He sailed across from Denmark with a fleet of sixty dragon ships to claim his inheritance, but died two years later whilst drinking at a wedding feast.'

Macaulay shook his head and gave a sigh.

'Nothing remarkable about those two,' he said, 'and after them came a weakling called Edward the Confessor.'

Nobody responded to this rather harsh judgment. Over to my left I could see Swift lying back in his armchair with his legs outstretched and his eyes closed. He looked as though he was fast asleep, but I knew he probably wasn't; this was a posture he often adopted during the quieter episodes. Hogarth, meanwhile, was gazing into the fire.

Macaulay resumed his narrative.

'Peace had brought prosperity, and there were many who now desired a slice of England, or possibly even the crown itself. These included several troublesome Welsh princes, the kings of Scotland, Norway and Denmark, and, lastly, Duke William of Normandy.'

'A storm approaching,' said Swift, without opening his eyes.

'As the pressure mounted, King Edward yielded royal authority to his chief minister, Harold Godwinson, Earl of Wessex, who was determined to keep these predators at bay. Concerned about the state of the navy, Harold sailed around the coast on a tour of inspection, only to be blown off course by a squall, shipwrecked in Flanders, captured by a Flemish nobleman and handed over to William of Normandy, who detained him for several months. He wasn't released until he'd promised to help William seize the English crown, a promise he broke in 1066 by taking the crown for himself.'

In the armchair next to mine I was aware of Gerard stirring with expectation. He knew what was coming next and so did I. England in the late summer of 1066! With bated breath we awaited a vivid portrayal of Harold's rush northward to fend off an invasion by

Vikings; his desperate march south again to oppose William; and his eventual defeat at the Battle of Hastings. I was mildly surprised, therefore, when Macaulay gave only a brief summary.

'You all know what happened,' he said. 'William attacked at nine o'clock on a Saturday morning before the English were ready. Needless to say, they didn't stand a chance.'

Macaulay's tone of voice suggested that there was a degree of unfairness in all this; that William had been somehow underhand in his timing; and that the English defeat had been thoroughly undeserved. There was more to come.

'Peace was a notion that William failed to understand. He had lived a violent life, and when he came to England he brought violence with him. Moreover, he misunderstood the people he'd conquered. He entered London in triumph, his massed troops watched by sullen crowds of spectators, and was crowned at Westminster Abbey on Christmas Day. The ceremony took place in silence; but when the crown was placed on William's head, the assembled Englishmen gave a great shout of acclamation.'

Macaulay paused and glanced around him.

'Shall I continue?' he asked.

'Please do,' said Swift. 'We're all ears.'

'This great shout was a custom that went back many years; it was heard whenever a new king received his crown. Unfortunately, the Norman soldiers mistook the shout for a sign of insurrection. They went on the rampage, manhandling the English and setting fire to their houses; meanwhile William was hustled away to safety. He quickly concluded that further pacification was required.'

Now Macaulay rose to his feet.

'Note the word 'pacification',' he said. 'Not 'peace' and most definitely not 'tranquillity'. This process of pacification brought complete change from what had gone before. William declared that he now owned every inch of England by right of conquest; that every Englishman was subordinate to him; and that all the land would be divided amongst him and his barons. To this effect he began building huge stone castles to overawe his subjects. Those who resisted him were punished without mercy, his greatest ire being felt by the north of the country, which he ravaged to the point of devastation!'

All the time he was speaking, Macaulay had been pacing back and forth across the room, hands clasped behind his back. Now he came to an abrupt halt, turned to face us and spoke in a voice quivering with indignation.

'And William had the effrontery to call it the king's peace!'

We watched as he strode to his armchair and slumped down, before reaching for the glass on the table beside him. The glass was empty.

'Allow me,' said Gerard, quickly rising to his feet to retrieve a bottle of port from the dresser. A few moments later he was replenishing Macaulay's glass; then everyone else's (Swift was now sitting upright again).

'Ah, that's better,' said Macaulay. 'Thank you.'

Before returning to his chair, Gerard made a bit of a show of examining the label on the bottle, as though it held some significance for him. I suspected he was building up to something, but in the end he merely placed the bottle back on the dresser and sat down again.

Helped by a glass of port, Macaulay's sense of outrage appeared to have subsided a little. He leant back in his armchair and informed us that the English people weren't the only ones to suffer under William the Conqueror.

'He also had three sons whom he bullied incessantly. The eldest was called Robert, but his father always referred to him as 'Curthose' (meaning short trousers) on account of his stature. The constant humiliation became too much for Robert and eventually he rebelled and fled to France.'

At this point I noticed a slight smile cross Macaulay's face; it was hardly anything and lasted only a brief moment, but it was there alright, and I realized he was quite pleased about something.

'Interestingly,' he said, 'Robert Curthose was the only person ever to unhorse William in single combat. The incident happened during a skirmish and William ended up lying in the mud. Robert apologized at once to his father and helped him remount before riding away. He later claimed he hadn't recognized him beneath his helmet.'

'A likely story,' said Swift. 'He probably did it on purpose.'

'Let's hope so,' said Macaulay.

8.

One afternoon I was leafing through my collection of 'LOOK AND LEARN' magazines when I came upon a striking picture. It was a full-page colour illustration of King William Rufus lying dead in a forest with an arrow sticking in him. I showed the picture to Gerard.

'It's what he's famous for,' I said, 'being shot dead in the forest whilst hunting deer.'

'Rather unlucky,' said Gerard. 'How did that happen?'

'Nobody knows' I replied. 'It looked like an accident, but most people suspected his brother Henry was behind it.'

'Sounds as if you've been reading ahead.'

'Yes, I have. Apparently Henry galloped off to the royal treasury and seized it at swordpoint. A few days later he was crowned King of England.' Sure enough, the next edition of 'LOOK AND LEARN' had a picture of Henry seizing the royal treasury at swordpoint.

'So what became of England at peace?'

'Good question,' I said. 'Macaulay's going to have his work cut out in the next few episodes.'

'Got very irate about William the Conqueror, didn't he?'

'You can say that again; it's almost as if he dislikes him personally.'

'William's sons don't sound any better.'

'They weren't,' I said, 'and his granddaughter Matilda was even worse.'

9.

'Dreadful woman,' said Macaulay. 'Kept her cousin imprisoned in chains.'

He was telling us about the struggle between Stephen and Matilda.

'It went on for years on end,' he continued. 'Two cousins battling for the crown. First one would get the upper hand, then the other. Meanwhile, there was anarchy throughout the land; robber barons building illegal castles; herds of livestock driven away; crops unharvested; peasants impoverished; nineteen winters of misgovernment all told. The haughty Matilda cared little about any of this. She was a cruel and vindictive woman who only sought to turn the chaos to her advantage. Stephen, by contrast, was gallant, merciful and chivalrous.'

'The type who'd stand his round down the pub,' said Gerard.

Macaulay ceased speaking and peered across the room.

Hogarth, I noticed, had looked up in surprise, and I expected Gerard's flippant remark to earn a reprimand at the very least; after all, he'd completely lowered the tone of the conversation. Instead, Macaulay furrowed his brow.

'You mean a public house?' he enquired.

'Yes,' said Gerard.

'Hmm,' said Macaulay. 'An interesting analogy.'

Hogarth examined his glass of port.

'Haven't been to a public house for years,' he said. 'Not since Cromwell closed them all down.'

'The scoundrel,' added Swift.

Gerard and I glanced quickly at one another.

'No, no,' I said, 'they're all still open, I can assure you of that.'

'Good grief,' uttered Hogarth.

A stunned silence followed. All three of them appeared visibly shaken by the revelation.

'Well, it's the first we've heard about it,' said Macaulay at length. 'Since when precisely?'

'As far back as I can remember.'

'After Cromwell?'

'Presumably, yes.'

'This is catastrophic,' said Swift with dismay. 'Why on earth weren't we informed?'

10.

'They should be here at seven o'clock,' I said. 'I thought it would be best to get a table early before the rush.'

'Good idea,' said Gerard. 'Shall we go in?'

'No, we'd better wait outside. Don't forget, this is their first time for quite a while.'

'Alright, as long as they're not late.'

It was a cold January evening with no moon. Pale lights shone through windows of frosted glass. Above our heads hung a sign depicting an oak tree in full leaf.

'Hope they don't get lost,' I said. 'I drew them a map, but it wasn't really to scale.'

'Here they come now,' said Gerard.

We could hear faint voices approaching, and a moment later Macaulay, Hogarth and Swift emerged from the gloom. They paused to gaze up at the sign, which was swinging gently back and forth in the breeze.

'The Royal Oak,' said Macaulay, by way of greeting. 'Tory house, is it?'

'Not really,' said Gerard.

'Can't be Whiggish.'

'It's neither of those,' I said. 'It's just the name of the pub, that's all. There's a place further up the road called the Parliament Tavern, but it's hardly different to this.'

I pushed open the door and led the way inside. My plan was for the five of us to sit around the large table near the fireplace, so I was pleased to see it was unoccupied.

'Rather a dark house,' remarked Macaulay, as he studied the sparse array of shaded lamps.

'Pubs don't go in for bright lights these days,' I said. 'Helps hide the dirt.'

'Grubby, is it?' said Hogarth. 'On close inspection?'

'Only slightly,' said Gerard. 'Now what would you like to drink?'

After a brief discussion it was agreed that our guests would all have Guinness, so Gerard went to the bar to do the honours. Meanwhile, the rest of us took our places at the table.

'Whose idea was that?' demanded Swift, pointing to a 'NO SMOKING' notice on the wall.

'A man called Benn,' I replied. 'It's gone and put half the pubs out of business actually.'

'I thought you said they were all still open.'

'Well, half are.'

'And this man called Benn. Roundhead, is he?'

'Kind of, yes.'

'I can just imagine,' he said. 'We know the type.'

Gerard returned with a trayful of glasses, and I watched with interest as Macaulay, Hogarth and Swift were each handed a pint of Guinness.

'Let it stand for a minute or two,' Gerard advised. 'It's better if you give it time to settle.'

They sat waiting patiently for a minute, and then another, and then we all took a drink.

'Ah,' said Swift with satisfaction. 'Reminds me of my childhood.'

Now that we'd broken the ice, so to speak, I decided to ask a question that had been lurking at the back of my mind for some weeks, but which I'd never got around to asking. I addressed it to Macaulay.

'You know the story of England at peace?'

'Yes,' he said. 'Of course.'

'I was wondering,' I said. 'Will there be any muffled oars?'

Macaulay squinted at me across the table.

'How do you mean?' he asked.

'Well,' I said, 'there seem to be a lot of boats involved in one way or another; you know, King Edgar going up the river, Canute being rowed to an island and so on; and I thought there might perhaps be somebody arriving secretly, or leaving maybe, in a boat with muffled oars.'

'Have you been reading ahead?'

'No, no,' I said. 'I just wondered, that's all.'

Macaulay pondered my query for a few moments.

'Well, there is a daring escape,' he said, 'but not in a boat.'

'Oh, yes?'

'It happened in 1142 when Matilda was besieged at Oxford. There was a heavy snowstorm at Christmas, so she dressed all in white and had herself lowered on ropes down the castle walls.'

'Blimey.'

'She got clean away.'

'Yes,' I said, 'that's the kind of thing I mean.'

Macaulay nodded. 'Thought so.'

'But preferably in boats with muffled oars.'

'No,' he said, 'there are no more boats, with or without muffled oars. Not for a good while anyway.'

'What about ships, though?' suggested Hogarth. 'They must play a part. After all, we're a maritime people.'

'Ships, yes,' said Macaulay. 'Sweyn Forkbeard came here in a ship. So did Canute, Hardicanute, Edward the Confessor, William the

Conqueror, William Rufus, Stephen, Matilda and Henry Plantagenet. All foreigners, of course.'

'Really?' I said. 'I never realized.'

'Danes, Normans, Angevins. The last lot didn't even call England by its proper name.'

'What did they call it then?'

"Angleterre'.'

'Confounded cheek!' said Hogarth.

Macaulay and Swift looked equally incensed, and I felt it was all my fault for raising the subject in the first place. Luckily, Josephine rode to the rescue. She was collecting empty glasses, and when she passed our table she paused and smiled at Macaulay, Hogarth and Swift.

'I like your coats,' she said.

They all glanced at their garments with surprise, as though they'd never noticed them before.

'Oh,' said Macaulay. 'Thank you.'

'And your shoes,' she added. 'Lovely buckles.' Josephine had an eye for these details. 'Where did you get them?'

This time it was Swift who answered.

'We've always had them,' he replied.

Josephine was too busy for further questions. The evening rush had now begun in earnest and the pub was starting to fill up rapidly with rowdy drinkers. She smiled again and collected a handful of empties before returning to her usual place behind the bar. I decided to buy another round before it got too hectic, so I went over and ordered five pints of Guinness. As I waited to be served, I turned and looked across at my companions. I was pleased to see Macaulay, Swift and Gerard deep in conversation. Judging from their expressions, it must have been a matter of great importance. Hogarth, meanwhile, sat slightly aloof, seemingly fascinated by the stream of drunken revellers swirling all around him.

11.

'By 1154,' said Macaulay, 'the robber barons held sway throughout the land. It was imperative they were brought to book, and Henry Plantagenet was just the man for the job. He took great delight in demolishing their castles; he made sure they paid their taxes; and for the time being he kept them in check.'

'Peace restored?' enquired Swift.

'Not quite,' came the reply. 'There was another fellow called Thomas à Becket who refused to submit. He was the king's former Chancellor and believed he was above the law.'

'Nobody's above the law.'

'Correct,' said Macaulay. 'So the king sent some knights to teach him a lesson.'

'Oh yes,' said Gerard, 'it turned nasty, didn't it?'

'Very nasty indeed, but we won't go into the details.'

This was a trait I admired in Macaulay. I'd noticed over the past few weeks that he never described brutal murders, gruesome executions, bloody reprisals and so forth, presumably because they jarred with his vision of England at peace. Instead he gave them only a passing reference. Likewise, there were certain monarchs who only received a cursory mention, and to whose fate he appeared entirely indifferent. A perfect example was Richard the Lionheart.

'Nothing but a public nuisance,' declared Macaulay. 'He went off to fight the Saracens, but then managed to get himself taken hostage. It cost a fortune to pay the ransom and set him free. Practically ruined the country, yet all he did was go off fighting again. He finally got shot by a crossbow whilst galloping around a besieged castle.'

'Served him right,' said Swift.

'Indeed.'

Macaulay fell silent for a moment, and I took the opportunity to read again the words inscribed on the wall above the fireplace:

CONSIDER HISTORY, WITH THE BEGINNINGS OF IT STRETCHING DIMLY INTO THE REMOTE TIME, EMERGING DARKLY OUT OF THE MYSTERIOUS ETERNITY: THE TRUE EPIC POEM AND UNIVERSAL DIVINE SCRIPTURE.

It occurred to me that the 'remote time' wasn't quite as remote as it had been a few weeks ago. Nonetheless, a great deal of history still lay ahead of us. Fortunately there had been many chroniclers down the years who'd gone to the trouble of recording the events of their day, and whose work was augmented by Macaulay's vast wealth of knowledge. He was so well-informed that he gave the impression of having met some of the protagonists in person, or at least somebody who'd met them. I was less certain about Hogarth and Swift. There were odd occasions when they seemed as astonished as I was by some particular outcome, but at other times I suspected they were fully aware of what would happen next. Of course, it was possible they'd already heard the entire story from start to finish and were simply refreshing their memories. As I said earlier, for all we knew they might have been in that room forever (except, that is, when they came to the pub with Gerard and me).

Macaulay now began speaking again.

'Imagine if you will,' he said, 'a pleasant meadow close to the River Thames on a summer's day. In the background we see colourful tents and pavilions with pennons flying, and before them sits a king. He is seated at a table, carefully signing a document, while standing all around him are noblemen and royal officials. A vision of peace and dignity, is it not?'

'Yes,' said Gerard.

'Well, I can assure you it was quite the opposite. The assembled noblemen were the robber barons I've been telling you about, and the king in question was so villainous he made them look respectable. He was only there because he'd run out of money.'

While Macaulay was talking I gradually realized that his description matched exactly the one in my 'LOOK AND LEARN'. It was a full-page colour illustration and showed King John signing the

Magna Carta, which granted liberty and justice to the English people. Vaguely I wondered if Macaulay had ever seen the picture, but then I quickly dismissed the thought as utterly foolish. After all, Macaulay was a highbrow, erudite scholar who'd probably never heard of 'LOOK AND LEARN'. The image he'd conjured up reflected the popular idea of Magna Carta, and had been reproduced in many forms throughout the years. Even so, it was a stirring depiction and I was disappointed to learn it wasn't completely true.

'He only signed it because they forced him to,' said Macaulay, 'and as soon as he had the chance he reneged on all his promises.'

12.

'Five glasses of Guinness,' said Swift, 'if you please.'

We were sitting at the same large table as before, and Swift made his request to Josephine when she came around collecting empties.

'It doesn't work like that,' she said. 'You have to come over to the bar and place an order.'

'Oh,'

We watched as a bewildered Swift stood up and made his way towards the press of people who were gathered near the bar. He waited a moment, then began squeezing himself into a suitable gap.

'Could be quite some time,' I remarked.

Luckily, both Gerard and I still had half-full glasses (we'd been drinking considerably more slowly than Macaulay, Hogarth and Swift, who'd all drained theirs a while ago).

'What do you think of the Guinness?' enquired Gerard.

'A fine porter,' replied Hogarth. 'Reminds me of my childhood.'

'That's just what Swift said.'

'Oh, really? I didn't hear him.'

It came as no surprise that Hogarth hadn't heard him. He appeared to be constantly distracted by the ribald goings-on at the Royal Oak and barely listened to any of our conversation. Not that he disapproved, I might add; seemingly it was the bawdier the better as far as he was concerned. He just sat there with a hazy look of contentment on his face.

Macaulay, meanwhile, showed no objection to the place, even though it hardly reflected 'England at peace'.

Or perhaps, on second thoughts, it did; after all, the general mood was invariably agreeable; there was never any trouble in the Royal Oak; arguments and disagreements maybe, but I couldn't recall there ever being any major unpleasantness; and definitely no punch-ups.

This evening, however, I sensed that Macaulay was slightly troubled about something. At first I assumed he was still seething about King John's evil deeds, but then I noticed him fumbling in his coat pocket, from which he withdrew a few silver coins. He gave these a brief examination and then put them back again; finally he peered across towards the bar where Swift had vanished from sight several minutes earlier.

Macaulay continued to look unsettled, and I was about to ask if anything was bothering him when Swift suddenly emerged from the crowd. He was bearing a tray laden with five pints of Guinness and appeared positively triumphant.

'That was hard work,' he said. 'Glad it's not my turn again for a while.'

Swift dispensed the glasses around the table, and as he did so Macaulay regained his former composure. His misgivings, whatever their cause, had evidently subsided.

Gerard now took the opportunity to finish off his previous pint, which he'd been carefully nursing in case Swift failed to return with a replacement.

'Not that I didn't trust him,' he told me later, 'but you never know.'

He was referring to the question of whose turn it was to buy a round. Up to this evening, Gerard and I had been fairly generous with Macaulay, Hogarth and Swift, having each stood them three lots of drinks apiece. We'd then decided that enough was enough and that one of them should pay, so we deliberately held back while they drained their glasses. As it turned out, Swift had bought the next round unprompted (apart from receiving procedural instructions from Josephine) and we now concluded they'd got the hang of it.

On the other hand, we needed to remember that the three of them were our guests. With this in mind, Gerard and I agreed not to enforce the buying of rounds too strictly. Just as long as they offered from time to time, it would be quite acceptable.

'After all,' I said, 'whenever we're in Macaulay's room we're given endless glasses of port.'

'Yes,' said Gerard, 'but I doubt if they've been out and bought it.'

'Where do you suppose it comes from then?'

'Well,' he said, 'it's probably always been there, just like they have.'

13.

'King John was not finished yet,' said Macaulay, 'and he made one last attempt to overthrow the barons. He took the remainder of the royal treasure and headed north through East Anglia with his baggage train. When he reached the Wash he found that the tide was out, so he decided to risk a crossing. This turned out to be a gross misjudgement and the entire baggage train was lost in the rising waters.'

As I listened to the latest instalment of 'England at peace', I found myself wondering whether it was indeed Macaulay's room we were all sitting in. The inscription on the wall suggested it was, but there again the same argument could equally apply to Hogarth and Swift. They all spent their time 'considering history' etc. etc. Or perhaps the room belonged to some venerable institution which had simply forgotten the three of them were there. Personally, I thought this was the most likely explanation. For convenience, however, Gerard and I continued to refer to it as Macaulay's room.

I was snapped out of my reverie when I realized he'd moved on to the next king.

'Henry the Indolent,' he said, 'endured similar struggles with the barons. They held him in captivity and forced him to call regular parliaments.'

At this point Hogarth raised his hand.

'Are there no tranquil interludes?' he asked. 'We haven't had any for ages.'

'I'm afraid not,' replied Macaulay.

'Pity,' said Hogarth. 'I enjoy your descriptions.'

'And me,' I said. 'It's the main reason I come here.'

Macaulay turned and looked at me with mild surprise.

'Is it really?' he said. 'I didn't realize.'

'Needless to say,' I added quickly, 'I'm interested in the rest of the story just as much.'

He acknowledged my remark with a nod.

'Well, I'm sorry to tell you,' he said, 'that the birth of parliament was a barbarous affair.'

14.

There was a sign behind the bar at the Royal Oak which said: **PLEASE DO NOT ASK FOR CREDIT AS A REFUSAL OFTEN OFFENDS.**

This was the law as far as I was concerned; nobody asked Josephine for credit because nobody dared; and the sign was merely for the uninitiated. I was disconcerted, therefore, when Josephine beckoned me to the end of the counter while I was ordering drinks.

'Just a quiet word,' she said, her voice cutting clearly through the surrounding hubbub. 'Your friends seem to have run up rather a large slate over the past few weeks.'

I stared at her in shock.

'You mean Macaulay, Hogarth and Swift?'

'Yes.'

'Well, how did that happen?' I said. 'You never give credit.'

'A moment of weakness,' she replied. 'They looked like ducks out of water so I gave them the benefit of the doubt.'

'You're not blaming me then?'

'Oh yes,' she said, 'it's all your fault.'

I turned and gazed across at our table where Gerard was holding the fort against interlopers. Macaulay, Hogarth and Swift were yet to arrive, and Gerard was doing his best to retain three empty chairs for their use, as well as mine. I needed to get back with the drinks and help him out.

I glanced at Josephine.

'You know they're all experts on history?'

'Maybe they are,' she said, 'but they're hopeless at economics.'

'I don't think they've got any money,' I added. 'Not modern pounds and pence, anyway.'

'So I gather.'

'What do you suggest then?'

'There's only one solution,' said Josephine. 'They'll have to sing for their supper.'

'How do you mean?'

She gave me an icy smile.

'Oh,' she said, 'I'm sure you'll think of something.'

I paid for my drinks and returned quickly to join Gerard, who listened with mounting alarm as I explained the situation.

'How much do they owe?' he asked.

'Josephine didn't say,' I replied, 'but she's holding us responsible.'

'Blimey.'

Three shadows passed by the frosted window, and a moment later Macaulay, Hogarth and Swift appeared in the doorway.

'Don't let them buy any more drinks,' I said urgently. 'Not until we've sorted this out.'

It so happened that Hogarth was already heading for the bar, so Gerard moved rapidly to intercept him.

'Allow me,' he said. 'Guinness all round, is it?'

'Er, yes, thank you,' said Hogarth, 'but isn't it my turn?'

'Don't worry about that,' said Gerard. 'Grab yourself a chair.'

Hogarth obeyed and sat down with a bemused expression on his face. Macaulay and Swift were already in their usual places. Just in time, actually, because the place was beginning to get even busier.

'Doesn't it ever quieten down? enquired Macaulay.

'I'm afraid not,' I said. 'There are no quiet pubs around here.'

Indeed, it would have been helpful on this occasion if it had been a little quieter. I was desperately trying to think of a way to approach Macaulay and the others on the question of their outstanding debt to the Royal Oak. At the same time I was attempting to fathom out what Josephine meant when she suggested they could sing for their supper. I was still pondering all this when Gerard returned with a trayful of drinks.

'Here you are,' he said, handing them around before raising a toast. 'To England at peace.'

As the others clinked their glasses it struck me I was lucky to have a friend like Gerard at such a critical time.

'There are quite a few people coming down from upstairs,' he remarked. 'Must be some society tipping out.'

Of course! No wonder there'd been a sudden upsurge of customers in the Royal Oak! There was a function room upstairs where all kinds of clubs and societies met on a regular basis. The pub relied on these groups for extra trade and allowed them to use the room for free. Josephine had once told me that takings at the bar never failed to increase on evenings when the function room was in use, so the clubs and societies were always made welcome.

I wasn't sure what particular society this was, but they didn't make a very good impression on Macaulay, Hogarth and Swift. Just along from us was another table where three people were sitting, drinking and talking quietly amongst themselves. The table had two spare chairs, apparently unused, and a couple of the newcomers abruptly seized them and took them away to another part of the pub. Not so much as a 'by-your-leave', let alone please or thank you! The three occupants slowly shook their heads in disbelief, then resumed their conversation.

The entire incident had been witnessed close-up by my companions.

'Just the kind of thing,' said Macaulay, 'that Lewis would have done.'

Gerard and I glanced at one another with looks of incomprehension.

'No, sorry,' I said, at length, 'we don't know anyone called Lewis.'

'Lewis the Fourteenth of France,' murmured Swift. 'The Sun King.'

'Oh him!' I said. 'Yes, I'm with you now.'

'No consideration for anyone else,' Macaulay continued. 'No concept of 'give and take'. Always the aggressor.'

'So I've heard.'

'Did you know he planned to use Mediterranean galleys against our English men-of-war?'

'What?' said Gerard. 'You mean galleys rowed by slaves?'

'Yes.'

'But that's outrageous!'

'Preposterous, more like,' said Macaulay. 'They hardly got beyond the Straits of Gibraltar before they sank.'

With this sobering thought in mind, we all sat contemplating our beers. Once again I was astounded by Macaulay's wealth of knowledge, and I realized I was already looking forward to the next episode of 'England at peace.'

Just then some stragglers descended the stairs from the function room. I watched them casually as they gathered near the bar, and in those few moments an idea came to fruition. I turned to Macaulay.

'You know the story of 'England at peace?'

'Yes,' he said. 'Of course.'

'I was wondering,' I said. 'Is it a moveable feast?'

Macaulay peered at me.

'What on earth do you mean?'

'Well, actually, I mean.........is it transferable?'

15.

The following week a notice appeared on various hoardings, telegraph poles and lamp posts in the vicinity:

WEDNESDAY EVENING

9.30 PM

THE ROYAL OAK

PRESENTS

'ENGLAND AT PEACE'

A TALK BY

THOMAS BABINGTON MACAULAY

ALL WELCOME

Gerard helped me put the notices up, and when we'd finished we went to the pub for a well-earned pint.

'That should do the trick,' he announced. 'There'll be people flocking in from miles around.'

Gerard had always been an optimistic kind of person.

'Not so sure about that,' I said. 'We'll have to see.'

We weren't expecting Macaulay, Hogarth and Swift to join us on this occasion, but we were sitting at the same large table as usual. It gave us a good view of the additional notice we'd pinned up in the stairwell, so that we could see if anyone went and read it. So far, nobody had.

'Early days yet,' said Gerard.

Maybe so, but I was far from confident about the forthcoming event. Apart from convincing Macaulay and the others of the pressing need to pay back their debt, I was beginning to have my doubts about the potential audience. Macaulay was accustomed to addressing four or five highly-attuned listeners with an interest in the history of England, whereas the function room had space for thirty or forty people. What if they started chatting amongst themselves during the talk? Or asking pointless questions? Or trying to leave before he finished? The worst scenario of course, would be if nobody came at all. It was imperative the talk was well-attended; otherwise we'd have to face the wrath of

Josephine. A secondary qualm had entered the equation only recently, in that Gerard had taken it upon himself to act as moderator at the event. He'd decided that Macaulay would require assistance because he'd be speaking in an unfamiliar venue. From my point of view this felt entirely unnecessary, but I didn't have the heart to reject Gerard's proposition.

'We could have a question-and-answer session afterwards,' he added.

'Suppose so,' I said.

'And to make sure it goes smoothly we can plant Hogarth and Swift in the audience.'

'Yes, good idea.'

Privately I'd been puzzling about what roles Hogarth and Swift might play when Macaulay gave his talk. In the beginning I'd toyed with the notion of them helping at the door, guiding people to their seats and so forth, but on second thoughts I'd decided this was a bit below their status. On the other hand, I could hardly provide comfortable armchairs for the pair of them to lounge around in while they exchanged droll remarks. I'd been in rather a quandary, but now Gerard seemed to have resolved the problem. In fact it was a stroke of genius, and at last my concerns began to recede.

'Watch out,' said Gerard. 'We've got a likely punter.'

He nodded towards the stairwell, where a man stood appraising our notice over the rim of his spectacles. We both knew who it was. His name was Douglas, and not for the first time I wondered why he bothered wearing spectacles when he invariably peered over their rim. I was convinced it was an affectation he'd adopted to make him appear mildly professorial, whereas in reality he was a bullying know-all. Douglas was a regular at pub quizzes and frequently confronted the question-master when he didn't agree with some answer or other (he was even known to squabble with members of his own team). His other chief characteristic was his fervent nationalism, which fortunately only surfaced from time to time. For the most part, however, Douglas was good company, fairly generous when it came to buying rounds of drink, and therefore tolerated by those who knew him.

We watched as he moved from the notice board to the bar, where he apparently made enquires before being directed to us.

'Brace yourself,' I told Gerard. 'He's coming across.'

Next moment Douglas was standing over us with a pint of beer in his hand.

'It has to be England, doesn't it?' he declared.

'Evening, Douglas,' I said. 'Care to join us?'

He sat down and glowered at us over the rim of his spectacles before resuming his assault.

'England, England, England,' he said. 'Always the same.'

'But that's where we live,' replied Gerard.

Douglas glowered again.

'It may have escaped your attention,' he said, 'but we happen to live on an island.'

'Oh yes,' said Gerard. 'I forgot.'

'And that island comprises three distinct nations! You can't talk about England at peace and ignore the other two!'

It never ceased to amaze me how Douglas could work himself up into a froth so rapidly. A few minutes earlier he'd been enjoying a quiet pint in a corner of the Royal Oak; then by some chance he'd caught sight of our notice and now he was seated at our table seething with rage.

'Who paid the price?' he demanded. 'Who suffered while Englishmen slept soundly in their beds at night?'

'Other Englishmen?' I suggested.

'What?!'

'The peasantry,' I said. 'The men (and women, too, actually) who toiled from dawn till dusk so that a few lords and ladies could live a life of ease.'

'That's not what I meant at all!'

'A life of ease built on peace and prosperity,' I continued, now getting fully into my stride, 'and prosperity in England had arisen from the wool trade. As a matter of fact, English wool was the envy of the known world in the thirteenth century. The preponderance of sheep......'

'Alright!' snapped Douglas, seizing his pint and rising to his feet. 'I've heard enough!'

'Does this mean you won't be coming to the talk?' enquired Gerard.

'I certainly will be,' said Douglas, 'and this Macaulay fellow had better know what he's talking about!'

With that he turned and stomped away.

Gerard smiled to himself.

'That reminds me,' he said. 'I must start wearing my winter woollies.'

'Yes,' I agreed. 'Quite chilly out, isn't it?'

The log fire flickered.

'Not in here though,' said Gerard.

'No,' I said. 'Not in here.'

16.

I'm not certain why I dropped in at Macaulay's room on the Wednesday afternoon. Perhaps it was to reassure myself that the three of them would indeed turn up for the talk, now that Gerard and I had gone to the trouble of getting it organized. Or maybe I wanted to check that Macaulay approved of the format, especially since a question-and answers-session had been included. Whatever the reason for my visit, I found myself wandering along the corridor around about dusk, and as I approached the room I heard voices within. From what I could make out, it sounded as if Swift was reading from a list of names.

'Edward the Martyr?' he began.

'No,' said Macaulay.

'Uhtred, earl of Bamburgh?'

'No.'

'Eadric The Grasper?'

'No.'

'Earl Tostig?'

'No.'

'King Harold Hardraada?'

'No.'

'Earl Gyrth?'

'No.'

'Leofwine?'

'No.'

'Copsig, earl of Northumbria?'

'No.'

'He only lasted five weeks.'

'Unfortunate.'

'Osulf? Less than a six months, by the way.'

'No.'

'Edwin, earl of Mercia?'

'No.'

'Waltheof, son of Siward?'

'No.'

'Malcolm Canmore?'

'No.'

'That takes us to 1093,' said Swift, 'and they all played a part.'

'I know they did,' replied Macaulay, 'but I'm afraid we'll have to leave them all out.'

'For the usual reasons?'

'Indeed.'

'Who's next?' said Hogarth.

'Er...let me see,' said Swift. 'Ah, yes. Simon de Montfort?'

'No.'

'Dafydd ap Gruffudd?'

'No.'

'William Wallace?'

'No.'

As I stood listening I gradually realized that Swift was listing individuals who'd been murdered, executed or killed in battle; and what they all had in common was that they'd met their deaths on English soil. Intrigued by what I heard, I continued to eavesdrop.

'Piers Gaveston?' said Swift.

'No.'

'Hugh Despenser?'

'Definitely not for the squeamish,' said Macaulay.

'Edward the Second?'

'Even more so.'

As a matter of fact, I'd been wondering how Macaulay would deal with Edward the Second, whose ghastly demise in Berkeley Castle was well-known. Now, it seemed, I had the answer: Macaulay would simply miss him out, just the same as he intended to bypass all the others on the list. In this way he was able to perpetuate his vision of England enjoying a long and peaceful history. Those who disrupted the peace were to be played down (at least, that was how I interpreted it anyway). I was highly impressed. Up until now I'd had no idea how much care Macaulay took with his preparation.

'Rather a lot of names,' remarked Hogarth.

'Yes,' said Swift, 'and there are many more to come.'

'Do you think anyone will notice if we leave them out?'

'Probably not,' said Macaulay. 'Nobody's interested in violence, conspiracy, jealousy and greed.'

At that moment I turned and retreated quietly down the corridor.

17.

I didn't bother telling Gerard about the list of names. He was bound to be disappointed to learn of all the grim happenings that were being omitted from the narrative. Besides, he was far too busy getting ready for the expected hordes. He spent the early evening going up and down the stairs between the bar and the function room, assessing who might be attending the talk and arranging chairs accordingly. There were no tickets because the event was free, so it was sheer guesswork on Gerard's part; he simply looked at the assembled throng and tried to judge which of them (if any) were likely to join us at nine-thirty. They were an assorted bunch, but I was pleased to see Douglas among them, accompanied by a few of his acquaintances. When there was nothing left to do, Gerard and I went and sat at our usual table to await the arrival of Macaulay, Hogarth and Swift.

We'd resigned ourselves to having to buy their drinks, at least for the time being, in the vague hope that their finances would eventually be put on a level footing (although we had no idea how this would be achieved). We still weren't sure, of course, whether they'd even turn up. I have to admit that I remained slightly edgy until the three of them actually walked through the door at nine o'clock, which was our prearranged hour to meet. The sight of them in their tailcoats and buckled shoes was most reassuring, and while Gerard headed for the bar to order some Guinness, I ushered them to the table.

'All set?' I asked.

'Yes, thank you,' said Macaulay.

'Now, do you have any special requirements; a blackboard, for example, or perhaps a lectern?'

I knew for certain that we'd be unable to provide either of these items, but I deemed it proper to offer them anyway, just to be courteous. Naturally I was relieved when Macaulay declined.

'We'll be fine,' he said.

Gerard returned with the drinks and raised a toast to 'England at peace'. After that it was simply a matter of waiting for the time to tick around to nine-thirty. We all sat quietly at the table, each of us engaged in our own thoughts, and there was no small talk or banter. Over the next half-hour we noticed people beginning to drift upstairs to the function room, glasses in hand, and at about twenty past nine Gerard invited Hogarth and Swift to accompany him in the same direction.

'If you don't mind,' he explained, 'I'd like to place you strategically amongst the audience.'

They showed no objection to the plan, but after the three of them had gone Macaulay turned to me and said, 'Making rather a fuss, isn't he?'

'It's just a precaution,' I said, 'in case there aren't any decent questions from the floor.'

He raised his eyebrows.

'Well,' he said, 'I can assure you those two won't ask questions just for the sake of it.'

'Fair enough,' I replied; and then a secondary thought occurred to me. 'Oh, by the way, I think Gerard's going to say a few words of introduction before you begin.'

In hindsight I realize that Macaulay can't have heard me properly. Or perhaps he chose to ignore what I said. Anyhow, at nine-thirty prompt I led him upstairs into the function room, where about thirty people sat waiting on hard chairs. Facing them were two other chairs, one empty and one occupied by Gerard, who was plainly expecting Macaulay to sit down beside him. Instead, however, he strolled to the front and launched directly into his talk.

'In 1174,' he began, 'William the Lion, King of Scotland, crossed the border and invaded England. During the summer months his forces ravaged the north, raiding and pillaging with apparent impunity.'

As Macaulay spoke I slipped onto a chair near the doorway, and discovered that my immediate neighbour was Douglas. He was sitting bolt upright with his arms folded, listening attentively, though he did manage to give me a curt nod of acknowledgment.

Macaulay continued.

'On the morning of 13th July, William was taking breakfast at his encampment near Alnwick Castle. A heavy coastal fog lay across the land, but when suddenly it lifted the king found himself surrounded by an English army. He was swiftly captured and the remainder of his followers dispersed. So it was that a meteorological fluke had preserved the peace in England.'

Beside me I was aware of Douglas stirring slightly on his chair.

'The captive king was taken to Northampton, where he was paraded through the streets with his feet bound together beneath his horse. This was an act of calculated humiliation, and he wasn't allowed home until he'd submitted to the English crown.'

Douglas stirred again, and I sensed he was about to speak when Macaulay resumed.

'But if the English thought they could meddle in Scottish affairs,' he said, 'they were sorely mistaken. Edward Plantagenet tried and failed to impose himself as overlord of Scotland, but it brought him nothing but grief. He finally expired on the shores of Solway Firth.'

'Ho ho!' said Douglas, with undisguised glee. 'So much for the 'Hammer of the Scots'!'

Macaulay paused and peered at him intently.

'So much indeed,' he said, 'and the next Edward fared even worse. He was driven out of Scotland by Robert the Bruce.'

Macaulay went on to explain how the defeat at Bannockburn left the north of England exposed to further Scottish raids; how the Plantagenets brought all their troubles on themselves; and how their choice of 'favourites' at court won the resentment of the 'commoners' who began to demand a voice in parliament.

Douglas, meanwhile, sat with a broad smile on his face, delighting at every English failure at the hands of the Scots. These, I had to confess, were dealt with very fairly by Macaulay.

'If the English desired peace,' he concluded, 'they should have stayed away from Scotland.'

Douglas was in plain agreement.

'You're quite right,' he said, beaming with pride. 'They should have kept their hooters out.'

There was a brief round of applause from the audience. Macaulay sat down in the empty chair beside Gerard and I noticed he appeared slightly drained, as if all his energy had been channelled into denouncing the Plantagenets. It reminded me of the occasion when he'd slumped down in his armchair after vigorously decrying William the Conqueror. In such circumstances I doubted if he was in the mood to take questions from the floor. Gerard, however, seemed to have different ideas.

'Well, thank you for that,' he said. 'Now do we have any questions?'

Hogarth and Swift were apparently of the same opinion as me. Both of them remained silent in the hope that Macaulay would be spared these unnecessary rigours. Inevitably, though, there were some people who felt obliged to pose a question, just for the sake of it. One of them was Douglas.

'Is it true,' he asked, 'that Edward preferred building castles to living in them?'

'Which Edward?' enquired Macaulay.

'The First.'

'Yes.'

Evidently satisfied with this reply, Douglas nodded and reached for his beer glass, which he'd positioned carefully on the floor beneath his chair. The glass was three-quarters empty. So was mine. A glance at the clock told me the time was now almost ten to eleven. I wondered if Gerard was aware of this fact. Unfortunately he couldn't see the clock, which was on the wall behind him.

'Are there any more questions?' he asked.

Macaulay looked unenthusiastic.

After a delay, someone said, 'Wasn't Robert the Bruce actually English?'

'Anglo-Norman to be precise,' replied Macaulay. 'He held estates in Scotland but he was definitely no Highlander.'

Douglas bristled with fury at the implied insult, but this time he said nothing. Seemingly he'd realized that the pub would soon be closing and further argument would only cause delay.

Yet still Gerard persisted.

'Any more questions?' he asked.

'Oh, come on Gerard,' I murmured to myself. 'That's enough.'

I watched in dismay as a man in the front row raised his hand and asked the kind of question which could arguably take hours to answer: 'What lessons can be learnt from history?'

Someone behind me groaned (I think it was Swift) but at that moment a bell clanged loudly downstairs and we heard a cry from Josephine.

'Last orders at the bar please!'

The effect this had on Gerard was astonishing to observe. His eyes opened wide and his face became pale with shock. He turned and looked up at the clock in disbelief, then sprang to his feet and headed for the door. Within seconds he was bounding down the stairs, pursued by a surge of people caught up in the race for a final drink (including Douglas and me).

Macaulay, Hogarth and Swift remained behind, and we didn't see them again that evening.

18.

Next day we received a mild rebuke from Josephine.

'You really should look after your friends better,' she said. 'They were still sitting in the function room when I went up to turn the lights off.'

'What time was that?'

'Half past twelve.'

'Blimey.'

'They told me they thought you were coming back.'

'Sorry,' I said. 'Bit of an oversight on our behalf.'

'So it seems.'

'How were they?' enquired Gerard.

'Inconsolable,' replied Josephine. 'So I consoled them with a pint of Guinness apiece.'

'Good idea.'

'Then Macaulay told me all about this king who rowed some other kings up the river.'

'No,' I said. 'It was the other way around.'

'How do you mean?'

'The other kings rowed him up the river.'

'Oh, yes, that's right.'

'Edgar, his name was. He's Macaulay's favourite king and he set the benchmark for England at peace.'

'Nice of him.'

Josephine now took a ledger from a shelf behind her and opened it flat on the end of the bar.

'Anyway,' she continued, 'you'll be pleased to know that last night's talk was a success.'

'Great.'

'The takings were up by a quarter compared with a normal Wednesday, so if I allow Macaulay and Co. a notional two percent of the gross it reduces their debt to half the previous amount.'

She indicated a page where I could see upside down the names Macaulay, Hogarth and Swift opposite a row of numerals, some of which had since been crossed out.

(Josephine had a better head for figures than me, so I didn't question her calculation.)

'Another talk,' she added, 'and they should move into credit.'

Gerard suggested that it would help if any subsequent event was scheduled to begin at seven-thirty, so as to finish earlier and avoid a panic at closing time.

We all agreed on that.

'Righto,' I said. 'Tomorrow I'll drop in at Macaulay's room and let the three of them know the arrangements.'

19.

The following afternoon I approached along the corridor and heard Swift reading from the list again. I paused for a moment.

'Roger Mortimer,' he said. 'Earl of March?'

'No,' said Macaulay.

'Wat Tyler?'

'No.'

'Hotspur?'

'No.'

'Warwick the Kingmaker?'

'No.'

'Henry the Sixth?'

'No.'

'Edward the Fifth?'

'No.'

'Richard the Crooked?'

'No.'

'Perkin Warbeck?'

'No.'

As I continued to listen it dawned on me that the grim roll-call had now advanced into the fifteenth century. History was flying along, with peace forever being interrupted by incidents of violence, intrigue, jealousy and greed. No wonder Macaulay found them so infuriating. At the same time I imagined it made him all the more determined to adhere to his chosen theme, which I for one found highly admirable.

I was still pondering all this when I suddenly realized that Macaulay's room had fallen silent. A few seconds later I heard a voice from within. It belonged to Hogarth.

'Is there anybody there?' he called.

'Sorry,' I said, moving quickly into the doorway. 'Only me.'

Whether they suspected me of eavesdropping I couldn't tell. The three of them peered at me without comment from their respective armchairs; then Macaulay gave me a nod and gestured for me to be seated. Swift, I noticed, was quietly folding away a sheet of paper.

'By the way,' I said, 'apologies for abandoning you the other night. No excuse for us all rushing off like that.'

'Well, we were rather taken aback,' replied Macaulay. 'It reminded me of the Retreat from Moscow.'

'Yes, I suppose it must have.'

Swift looked up abruptly.

'The Retreat from Moscow?' he said. 'I don't remember that.'

'No, you wouldn't,' replied Macaulay. 'It was after your time.'

'Mine too, I presume,' said Hogarth.

'I'm afraid so.'

I found this exchange slightly baffling, but I didn't say anything. Macaulay rose from his armchair and poured me a glass of port, from which I inferred that I was no longer in their bad books for deserting them. Even so, I knew I had to be a little more solicitous of their welfare in future, especially as we needed them back at the Royal Oak. I explained about the proposed second talk and the seven-thirty start.

'And it won't happen again,' I assured them.

'What won't?' said Swift.

'The Retreat from Moscow.'

20.

'I've been reading ahead,' announced Gerard, 'and there's an episode with muffled oars coming up.'

We were sitting at our usual table in the Royal Oak, awaiting the arrival of Macaulay, Hogarth and Swift.

'Don't tell me,' I said. 'You're referring to Roger Mortimer.'

'Yep,' said Gerard. 'He escaped from the Tower of London in a boat with muffled oars.'

'Then he ran off with Queen Isabella.'

'Oh, you knew already?'

'Certainly,' I said, 'and I can assure you that Macaulay won't be mentioning him.'

'But he practically ruled the country for three years!' Gerard protested. 'How can he not mention him?'

'Because he met a very sticky end.'

'What happened to him then?'

'I'd rather not say.'

It transpired that Gerard hadn't read very far ahead, at least not as far as me. I then told him about the list of proscribed names.

'As a general rule,' I said, 'anybody who was murdered, executed or killed in battle is either passed over or played down.'

'Well, Mortimer was definitely in the second category.'

'Indeed.'

'So there'll be no tales of muffled oars?'

'Not for a while anyway.'

Gerard puffed out his cheeks.

'Let me make sure I've got this right,' he said. 'It's a list of people who died violent deaths.'

'Correct.'

'Because of intrigue, jealousy and greed.'

'Mostly, yes.'

'But if there's no violence, intrigue, jealousy or greed,' he demanded, 'then what else is there?'

'Peace and tranquillity,' I replied. 'Boats being rowed along rivers, sheep grazing on hillsides; ships carrying bales of wool to foreign ports......'

I could have given more examples but just then three shadows passed by the frosted window and a moment later Macaulay, Hogarth and Swift appeared in the doorway.

Their entrance caused a bit of a stir. I'd been so involved in my conversation with Gerard that I'd remained totally oblivious to the other customers in the Royal Oak. A quick glance around told me the place had filled up considerably and, furthermore, it was plain that many had come especially to attend the talk. As Macaulay, Hogarth and Swift approached our table a discernible wave of expectancy passed amongst the bystanders, some of whom I noticed were wearing tailcoats with shiny buttons up the front. For the time being, though, they all kept a discreet distance.

It was my round, so I went off to buy the beers while Gerard secured some seats for our guests. There was quite a crush at the bar. Despite being a regular I didn't get served straightaway, and as I stood waiting I became aware of somebody pressing into the limited space beside me. It was Douglas. He appeared to be in a combative mood.

'England at peace still, is it?' he enquired.

'Yes,' I answered, 'as far as I know.'

'Ho ho,' he said. 'We'll see about that.'

'So I take it you're coming to the talk?'

'Try and stop me.'

When eventually I returned to our table I decided not to mention the encounter with Douglas. Besides, my companions were busy agreeing a format for the talk. Apparently Gerard had decided to step back from his role as moderator and allow Macaulay to deal with any questions himself.

'You don't need me to help fend them off,' he said, 'so I'll take a back seat if you don't mind.'

It seemed that Macaulay found this arrangement perfectly satisfactory, so at seven-twenty Gerard, Hogarth and Swift wandered upstairs to find themselves somewhere to sit, taking their pints with them. Meanwhile, I stayed behind to keep Macaulay company. We watched as another thirty or forty people slowly progressed towards the function room. Some of them glanced at Macaulay as they went by; others passed in respectful silence; and I couldn't help feeling rather pleased with myself that I'd discovered him first. My only concern was Douglas. Obviously the presence of somebody with such forthright opinions was welcome. I only hoped he wasn't planning to impose them on the rest of us. For some reason Macaulay hadn't yet touched his Guinness. Perhaps he was allowing a few more minutes for it to settle, but actually it looked perfect to me. His glass sat on the table between us and was full to the brim. Mine was already two-thirds empty; and gradually I began toying with the idea of buying a second pint to take into the talk. The problem was that the time was drawing critically close to seven-thirty. The bar was still fairly busy and I had serious doubts whether I'd get served quickly enough. Luckily, however, Macaulay seemed to have followed my stream of thoughts.

Suddenly he nodded at his Guinness and said, 'Would you like that?'

'Oh,' I said, with surprise. 'Don't you want it?'

'I can get another later,' he replied. 'You can have it, if you wish.'

'Oh, well,' I said. 'Yes, thanks, I will.'

I made a mental note to repay this act of generosity when the opportunity arose.

At last it was seven-thirty, so I led the way upstairs carrying my spare pint and just managed to grab one of the few empty seats in the function room. A chair had been placed at the front for Macaulay's sole use, but once again he chose to remain standing.

I'd barely sat down when he began delivering his talk.

'England is a naturally peaceful country,' he said. 'We never seek out enemies but on occasion we've attracted the envy of others. In 1340 the French became jealous of our burgeoning wool trade. They planned to blockade the English ports and therefore began assembling a vast fleet of warships in an estuary at Sluys in Flanders. When King Edward the Third learnt of this he assumed an invasion was imminent, so he decided to carry out a preventative raid. On the 24th of June he sailed across the Channel and attacked the French vessels, which had all been chained together to create a kind of floating fortress. Unable to escape, they were utterly destroyed.'

I glanced across at Douglas. He was sitting with his arms folded in his usual seat by the door and appeared to be paying very close attention. So far he'd shown no reaction to Macaulay's narrative, but nevertheless I sensed he was waiting for some opening into which he could pounce.

'The prospects of invasion were now remote,' said Macaulay, 'and henceforth the fighting would be confined to French soil. The rival kings were engaged in a war that was destined to last for more than a hundred years. They fought it out at Crécy, Poitiers and Agincourt but actually the impact of these battles was hardly felt in England, where peace and prosperity continued to flourish.'

Macaulay paused for a moment, at which point Douglas raised his hand.

'Excuse me for asking,' he said, 'but if England enjoyed all this peace and prosperity, why was there a peasants' revolt?' Douglas sat back with a look of self-satisfaction on his face. He'd submitted his query in a cool and polite manner, but he evidently felt he'd just produced a trump card from up his sleeve.

'A very good question,' said Macaulay, 'and you're absolutely right to broach the subject. As a matter of fact it wasn't just peasants who were involved, but also townspeople, craftsmen and minor officials. They'd heard about the Magna Carta and they wanted a share of the justice and liberty it was supposed to promise; they objected to paying a poll tax of a shilling a head; and they wished to see the end of serfdom. In due course King Richard the Second met the rebels at Smithfield and agreed to their demands. After they'd dispersed, however, he ordered the ringleaders to be rounded up and punished. This was a typical example of Plantagenet mendacity.'

All the while, Douglas had sat listening to the answer in forlorn silence, and I noticed he didn't appear quite as smug as he had before. If he'd been hoping to entrap or otherwise thwart Macaulay with his intervention he had most obviously failed.

'I don't like the Plantagenets,' was all he had to say.

'Neither do I,' said Macaulay. 'They were a bunch of villains who cared nothing for their people.'

'Nor their neighbours,' said Douglas.

'Indeed not,' came the reply. 'They imprisoned three Scottish kings and held them hostage for years; they built enormous castles in Wales without so much as a by-your-leave; and they trod all over the Irish.'

This list of indictments seemed to appease Douglas. He nodded his assent and for the remainder of the talk asked no more awkward questions. In fact I got the impression that Macaulay had completely won him over. During the evening his manner slowly transformed from quarrelsome to acquiescent; and I concluded we should have no further concerns about him.

Only later did I discover how wrong I was.

21.

'Gentlemen, you are now in credit at the bar,' said Josephine. 'What can I get you?'

We were sitting at our usual table and she addressed her enquiry to Macaulay, Hogarth and Swift. Before us were five empty glasses.

'Actually,' said Macaulay, 'I've had quite enough to drink for one evening.'

'Me too,' said Swift.

Gerard and I had organized the event, but apparently we were being offered nothing.

This left only Hogarth, who as usual was studying the antics of other customers at nearby tables. I was sure he would have liked to stay for another pint but he obviously realized he was out-voted.

'Not tonight,' he said. 'Thanks all the same.'

Soon the three of them were buttoning up their tailcoats and making ready to leave. It had been a successful evening. The Wars of the Roses had just broken out when Macaulay brought his talk to an end. Before that he'd told us about the overthrow of King Richard by the usurper Henry Bolingbroke; the further crushing of rebellion; and the rise to prominence of Bolingbroke's rather unpleasant son Henry the Fifth. Afterwards there were a few sensible questions from the audience and then we'd all adjourned downstairs. The only memorable exchange was when somebody in the front row asked Macaulay the names of the three Scottish kings who'd been imprisoned.

'John Balliol, David Bruce and James Stewart,' he replied, quick as a flash, and once again I couldn't help but be impressed by his depth of knowledge.

A glance at Douglas told me that he, too, knew the answer, but as I said before he spent the rest of the talk in the role of attentive listener only. On the way down the staircase I noticed him speaking briefly to Gerard; and then he merged into the milling throng at the far end of the bar.

I wasn't sure whether any future events were envisaged; the matter hadn't been discussed and the time wasn't appropriate anyway (it was almost ten to eleven). Macaulay seemed eager to return to the sanctuary of his room and as always his companions obliged. After we'd said goodnight to the three of them I sat staring at my empty glass, waiting for Gerard to realize it was his turn to buy a round. I thought he looked a little pensive and it was only after a minute or so that he rose to his feet and went off to get served. When he returned with the drinks he sat down quietly opposite me.

'Everything alright?' I asked.

'Yes,' he said, 'of course.'

That wasn't how it looked to me, so I decided to try a bit of light-hearted conversation.

'Did you see how Macaulay dealt with Douglas?' I remarked. 'What a professional.'

'Yes,' said Gerard.

'Not many people get the better of him.'

'No.'

'By the way,' I continued, 'I saw Douglas collar you on the stairway. What was that all about?'

'He was asking for some background details about Macaulay, Hogarth and Swift.'

'Oh yes?'

'I told him I knew very little.'

'Well done,' I said. 'The last thing we want is Douglas turning up at Macaulay's room.'

'Yes'

There was a pause; Gerard attempted a weak smile; and at that moment the truth dawned.

'Oh no!' I said. 'Don't say you've told him where it is!'

'Sorry,' replied Gerard, 'but he was very persistent. I only told him to get rid of him.'

It was pointless being cross with Gerard: the deed was done. We sat nursing our pints and considered the possible implications.

'Perhaps he's just interested in history,' Gerard suggested, 'like we are.'

'Maybe,' I said, 'but he's such a know-all there's probably nothing for him to learn.'

'But surely the thing about Macaulay is the way he tells it.'

'Suppose so,' I conceded, 'but I've got a feeling Douglas has other motives.'

'Such as?'

'Not sure,' I said, 'but we're going to have to keep an eye on him.'

22.

'The Wars of the Roses,' said Macaulay, 'were relatively peaceful. There were a few brutal encounters between various aristocrats and their retainers which may have caused a little local disruption; but for the most part the ordinary people remained exempt.'

I sat listening to Macaulay in fascination. Gerard and I had arrived at his room late in the afternoon on the following day and found him already in full flow. It came as a bit of a shock to discover he'd resumed his talks without us; and in that instant I realized that Macaulay's true audience comprised only Hogarth and Swift. By comparison, Gerard and I were mere dabblers who dipped into history from time to time. I'd learnt enough, however, to know that the Wars of the Roses had generated several decades of civil strife, the murder of two kings and the death in battle of a third, not to mention countless dukes, earls and knights. Yet Macaulay seemed to be dismissing all this as 'a little local disruption'.'

Apparently Swift shared my misgivings.

'Damned nuisance more like,' he remarked. 'All those Lancastrians and Yorkists galloping through people's crops.'

'Well, yes, when the battles took place they were a nuisance,' Macaulay concurred, 'but as I've mentioned before, the Plantagenets didn't care about anyone else.'

'Wouldn't it have been better just to get rid of them altogether?'

Macaulay adopted a grave expression.

'Which is exactly what happened,' he said. 'In the final battle everybody turned against Richard the Crooked and that was the end of him.'

'Bosworth Field,' uttered Gerard in a knowledgeable tone, 'the advent of the Tudors.'

At this juncture I would normally have expected Macaulay to peer at Gerard and enquire whether he'd been reading ahead. This afternoon, though, he offered a correction instead.

'As a matter of fact,' he announced, 'the Tudors dropped the family name fairly quickly. Henry Tudor claimed Welsh descent; he landed his forces in Wales and marched under the banner of the Red Dragon; but once he was king of England he tended to play down his Welsh connections. Henceforward he was known as Henry Rex the Seventh.'

'Presumably then,' I said, 'the Welsh received no special favours.'

'Even worse,' said Macaulay with disdain. 'Wales was simply absorbed under the English crown.'

He didn't look particularly pleased when he told us this, and I began to wonder if his opinion of the Tudors was any better than it was of the Plantagenets. Over the past few weeks it had become clear to me that Macaulay was hugely unimpressed by the majority of our kings and queens (the sole exception, of course, being the venerable Edgar). There again, it was necessary to bear in mind that his subject was not 'The kings and queens of England' but rather 'England at peace', which was entirely different. Plainly he recognized that if we treated our neighbours badly, then the prospects of peace were jeopardized;

hence his apologetic manner whenever he discussed Wales, Scotland or even Ireland.

Macaulay had fewer qualms, however, when championing English exploits upon the rolling deep.

'It was about this time,' he continued, 'that English sea power began to come of age. Under the Plantagenets we'd gained vast territories in France and swiftly lost them again; but by good fortune we'd obtained the keys to Calais and so we now commanded the Straits of Dover whichever way the wind blew. Our ships plied the waters of the English Channel, exporting wool, importing wine, policing foreign vessels and seizing unlicensed cargoes.'

Macaulay raised a finger.

'And before you ask,' he said, 'yes, there was a very fine distinction between legitimate trade, smuggling and outright piracy. We got around this difficulty by referring to our ships as 'privateers', a tradition encouraged in royal circles and maintained for many years.'

I'd noticed on previous occasions how Macaulay often included seafaring in his descriptions of England at peace. This seemed reasonable enough to me; after all, we were supposed to be a maritime people. Nonetheless, I was astonished that he was prepared to accept such blatant bending of the rules when it came to nautical matters. He went on to explain that England had no proper navy at the time; and that the privateers provided an invaluable service by protecting our coast from invasion; by establishing seaways to more distant lands; and by compiling information for rudimentary charts.

Yet it was a comment by Swift that revealed the true reason why these privateers were so readily tolerated.

'For Englishmen,' he said, 'the unfettered pursuit of trade has always been sacrosanct.'

'Trade, profit and prosperity,' added Hogarth. 'There is nothing more important.'

At these words, Macaulay leant back in his armchair, apparently content that today's talk had reached a satisfactory conclusion. I had to confess I liked the way it had been neatly rounded off by Hogarth and Swift, who only ever intervened at appropriate times; and who never asked awkward or provocative questions. Once again I told myself there was little to compare with listening to Macaulay as he expounded his theory of England at peace. It was a historian's equivalent of heaven, all five of us had a glass of port at our side; the fire was roaring in the hearth and a general air of tranquillity filled the room.

Heaven, that is, until Douglas appeared in the doorway. He was carrying a notebook and pencil.

Now, the practise Gerard and I always adopted when we arrived at Macaulay's room was to stand waiting politely outside until we were 'nodded in' by our host; then we would move to our allotted armchairs, courteously acknowledging Hogarth and Swift before sitting down.

Not so Douglas.

'Hope I haven't missed anything,' he said cheerily, striding inside and warming himself in front of the fire.

'Cold out,' he remarked.

Oddly enough, Macaulay and the others didn't seem particularly surprised to see him. They gave him the same unfathomable look they'd given me when I'd been eavesdropping outside the door; then Hogarth indicated a hard chair in the corner of the room (there were no spare armchairs). As Douglas sat down I noticed he made a point of ignoring Gerard and me. Instead, he opened his notebook and held his pencil at the ready.

'It so happens,' said Macaulay, 'that you've missed the entire talk.'

'Ah,' replied Douglas.

'But I suppose there'll be no harm if we go over it again, just as long as nobody minds?'

Hogarth and Swift said nothing; neither did Gerard, so it was left to me to answer the question.

'No, no,' I said, 'we don't mind at all.'

'Good.'

Macaulay sat upright in his chair; then he collected his thoughts for a few moments before speaking.

'The Wars of the Roses,' he said at length, 'were relatively peaceful. There were a few brutal encounters between various aristocrats and their retainers which may have caused a little local disruption; but for the most part the ordinary people remained exempt.'

'Damned nuisance,' said Swift. 'All those Lancastrians and Yorkists galloping through people's crops.'

23.

'You know Macaulay's list?' said Gerard. 'The people who died violent deaths who he avoids mentioning?'

'Yes,' I replied.

'What's he going to do when he gets to Anne Boleyn?'

'How do you mean?'

'Well, he can hardly miss her out, can he? It's the most famous beheading in history.'

'Perhaps he'll skirt around her,' I suggested, 'or maybe just mention her in passing.'

'Suppose so.'

'After all, he mentioned Richard the Third in the last talk, and he was definitely on the list.'

'Was that Richard the Crooked?'

'Yes.'

'But he deserved death!' protested Gerard. 'Anne Boleyn didn't!'

I was rather taken aback by Gerard's highly judgmental stance.

'Blimey,' I murmured. 'I hope you're never on a jury.'

Even so, he'd raised a valid point. Now that we'd entered the Tudor period there were countless executions and judicial murders lying ahead of us (though it should also be mentioned that we could expect fewer battles). Actually I'd been wondering for a while how Macaulay planned to navigate these increasingly choppy waters.

Apparently, Gerard also had his doubts.

'Anne Boleyn is merely the tip of the iceberg,' I said. 'There's also Catherine Howard, Lady Jane Grey and Mary Queen of Scots.'

'Oh, yes,' said Gerard. 'I'd forgotten all about them.'

We were sitting at our usual table in the Royal Oak on the Monday of the following week, pondering the future of England at peace.

'If it's any consolation,' I ventured, 'Henry the Eighth only beheaded two of his wives.'

'Yes, but the other four had to live with him,' said Gerard. 'That was probably worse.'

Just then the door opened and a man I vaguely recognized came into the pub. He was wearing a tailcoat with shiny buttons up the front; also a pair of buckled shoes. We watched as he headed directly into the stairwell, where he stood for several moments examining the notice board. Next he went around to the bar and spoke briefly to Terence, who handed him a yellow ticket in exchange for a five pound note (it was Josephine's evening off). The newcomer didn't stop for a drink and a minute later he was gone.

'Fancy outfit,' remarked Gerard. 'Looks as though we've started a fashion.'

'Possibly,' I said. 'Now where have I seen him before?'

'He came to the talk the other week with Douglas.'

'Oh, yes, that's right.'

'He asked that ridiculous question about what lessons could be learnt from history.'

It was Gerard's turn to buy a round, so he went over to the bar, helpfully taking our empty glasses with him. Meanwhile, I gazed idly at the other drinkers scattered at various tables here and there. I noticed that roughly half of them were wearing tailcoats with shiny buttons up the front; apparently, Gerard's observation had been quite correct. I pictured the man who'd just departed; he, too, had been wearing a tailcoat. In the same instant a chilling thought occurred to me. I sprang to my feet and marched through to the stairwell, where I saw immediately that a brand new poster had been pinned up:

THE ROYAL OAK

PRESENTS

'THE PEACE TALKS'

BY

THOMAS BABINGTON MACAULAY

EVERY WEDNESDAY AT 7.30 PM

TICKETS £5

BOOK NOW

When Gerard returned with the drinks I sent him over to see the poster for himself. He came back looking most indignant.

'I bet Douglas is behind this,' he said. 'Yes, most likely,' I agreed.

'That's probably why he hung around when we were leaving last week. Do you remember, he stayed chatting to Macaulay and the others? I thought he was up to something.'

Clearly we had no evidence that Douglas had arranged the new series of talks, but he was the most obvious suspect; Josephine's temporary absence meant we couldn't ask her what she knew about it, though without doubt she must have given her approval; and they'd even had the audacity to charge five pounds a ticket; all of which left Gerard and me feeling rather aggrieved.

'We've been hijacked,' I said. 'Macaulay belongs to us. We discovered him, not Douglas.'

'And why've they been changed to 'peace talks'?' demanded Gerard.

'I suppose somebody must have decided to jazz them up a bit.'

'Outrageous.'

'I only hope Macaulay knows what he's getting involved with.'

24.

By the next afternoon copies of the same poster had appeared at various other locations in the vicinity. Pasted onto hoardings, telegraph poles and lamp posts, they now carried an additional strapline:

DON'T BOTHER COMING IF YOU'RE NOT INTERESTED IN HISTORY

'Rather aggressive,' said Gerard. 'Hardly in keeping with the idea of England at peace.' We saw the posters on our way to visit Macaulay, having decided overnight that we should at least sound him out about the talks. At the same time we were fully aware that a little circumspection was required; after all, he might have been completely at ease with the way they were being promoted. We just wanted to make sure.

'Probably best not to mention the posters,' I said. 'Not for the moment anyway.'

'No,' said Gerard.

'We'll just turn up as normal, settle into our usual chairs and see what happens.'

However, when we arrived at Macaulay's room we found the door was closed.

We knocked and waited, then knocked again before cautiously looking inside. The room was quite empty. Some embers glowing in the fireplace told us it had been only recently deserted, but we were at a loss as to where the three of them could have gone.

'You don't think they're trying another pub, do you?' said Gerard. 'I know they were curious about the Parliament Tavern.'

'I doubt it,' I replied. 'Don't forget they haven't got any money.'

'Oh, no, I forgot,' he said. 'So that rules out the shops too'.

'And the bank.'

'Yes.'

We stood for a few seconds, pondering in silence, then Gerard had a spark of inspiration.

'Maybe they've gone to the park,' he said. 'It's only over the road.'

'What would they go there for?'

'Well, it's fairly gloomy in here without any windows. Perhaps they fancied a change.'

For want of a better suggestion we retraced our steps back along the corridor, through a maze of other corridors and hallways, then finally down a flight of steps and out into the daylight. On the opposite side of the road lay a large stretch of parkland.

'Haven't been here for years,' I said, as we headed through the wrought iron gates.

'No, nor me,' said Gerard.

We wandered past a row of green benches in the vague hope of finding the three comrades engaged in deep discussion, but they were all empty. When we reached the final bench we sat down and gazed across the grassy expanse. There were large trees dotted here and there, just beginning to come into leaf, and beyond them was a shimmering lake. A distant figure stood alone at the water's edge.

'Isn't that Swift?' asked Gerard, whose eyesight was considerably better than mine.

'Suppose it could be,' I said. 'What's he doing over there on his own?'

'Don't know.'

Gerard scanned the further reaches of the park and eventually spotted Hogarth too. He was in the middle of a large open space.

'They could hardly be more remote from one another, could they?' said a voice beside us. It belonged to Macaulay. Where he'd popped up from I had no inkling, but it took a few moments for Gerard and me to recover from the surprise.

Macaulay peered at us enquiringly, and I realized neither of us had answered his question.

'No, no,' I replied. 'They're a long way apart.'

'Indeed,' he said. 'Here we see demonstrated the situation in Europe in the summer of 1520. Over by the lake we have Swift, representing Charles V, emperor of Spain, Italy, Austria, Germany and the Netherlands; while beyond the trees stands Hogarth. His role is

Francis 1, king of France. The two of them, of course, were implacable enemies; and in consequence they each sought the friendship of a third player.'

'Henry the Eighth?' I ventured.

'Correct,' said Macaulay, before turning to Gerard. 'Would you mind being him?'

'No, I'd be delighted,' said Gerard. 'What do you want me to do?'

'Stand here and represent England,' came the instruction.

'Righto.'

Gerard stood up and gave a friendly wave to Hogarth and Swift, who both waved back.

'Now picture if you will,' continued Macaulay, 'a great field studded with gorgeous tents and pavilions; with pennants flying and wine flowing; and hundreds of horsemen and squires and armed retainers all gathered together in the name of peace. Such was the planned meeting between Henry and Francis at the Field of the Cloth of Gold.'

'Was that here?' I asked.

'No,' said Macaulay. 'It was in France.'

'Oh.'

'Unfortunately, a week before the meeting a complication arose when Charles decided to pay Henry a surprise visit. He was sailing through the Channel and landed at Dover just as Henry was about to leave for Calais. The timing could not have been worse.'

'But shouldn't that have made the chance of peace more likely,' I said, 'rather than less?'

'How do you mean?'

'Well, surely Henry could be friends with both Francis and Charles.'

'I'm afraid it didn't work like that,' said Macaulay. 'The balance of power meant he had to choose one or the other.'

'Oh, I see.'

'In the event he chose neither, and as a consequence England has been isolated ever since.'

I couldn't tell whether Macaulay viewed this as a good outcome or not. He merely regarded Gerard and me without expression for several long seconds before signalling to his friends that it was time to return. The lesson, apparently, was over. We watched Hogarth and Swift as they came sauntering back; then we all headed towards the park gates.

I was just wondering if we'd be invited to the room when we came upon a poster advertising the 'peace talks'.

Macaulay paused briefly to examine it.

'Oh, by the way,' he said. 'I assume you'll both be attending on Wednesday evening?'

'Yes, hope to,' replied Gerard.

'Then I'll arrange for you to be exempted from the entrance fee.'

'Thanks.'

The poster carried the new strapline:

DON'T BOTHER COMING IF YOU'RE NOT INTERESTED IN HISTORY

'Not sure about that though,' added Macaulay. 'Might have to have a word about it.'

He didn't say who he'd have to have a word with; and we didn't ask.

25.

The following afternoon, Gerard and I went to the Portrait Gallery. We thought it would be helpful if we saw what all these kings and queens we'd heard about actually looked like. Yet the first thing we noticed when we entered the section marked 'Tudors' was that it wasn't just kings and queens anymore. Now there were other participants as well: Chancellors, Lord Protectors, even Gentlemen of the Wardrobe, all influencing important events in England. Many of them appeared grander in their finery than the monarchs themselves (although most ultimately fell from grace).

On the opposite wall were portraits of the legendary seafarers: Frobisher, Hawkins, Drake and Raleigh. These were the 'privateers' that Macaulay had mentioned.

We stopped to have a look at Sir Francis Drake, posing in his doublet and hose.

'I'll bet he didn't wear that outfit when he went to sea,' remarked Gerard.

'No,' I said, 'probably not.'

'He'd never get up the rigging with those on.'

'No.'

Next along was Sir Walter Raleigh.

'I suppose you could say he captures the spirit of 'Merrie England'.'

'Why?' I asked.

'Well, you know, it was a rainy day so he took his cloak off and laid it in the mud for Good Queen Bess.'

'That's only half the story,' I said. 'Sir Walter was another person who came to a sticky end.'

'Oh, was he?'

'He'll definitely be on Macaulay's list.'

A little later we reached an entrance marked 'Stuarts'.

'Right,' I said. 'That's far enough for today.'

'Aren't we going in?' asked Gerard.

'No,' I replied. 'We don't want to get ahead of ourselves, do we?'

I studied Gerard's face as he considered my words.

'Blimey!' he exclaimed suddenly. 'What about.......?'

'I've no idea.'

'But you don't know what I'm going to ask!'

'Yes, I do,' I said, 'and I really think we should leave it for the time being.'

26.

When evening came we approached the Royal Oak warily. Obviously we were looking forward to Macaulay's latest talk, nevertheless, the idea of Douglas being in charge of affairs was rather disturbing. We arrived at 7.15 to find he'd already set himself up with a table and chair at the foot of the staircase, checking tickets and selling new ones to latecomers. He eyed Gerard and me offhandedly.

'Ah yes,' he said, 'I understand you're entitled to complimentary tickets.'

'Yes,' I answered.

He handed them over without further comment and we went through to the bar to get some drinks.

'Seen this?' said Gerard, indicating some words printed on the back of his ticket:

CONSIDER HISTORY, WITH THE BEGINNINGS OF IT STRETCHING DIMLY INTO THE REMOTE TIME, EMERGING DARKLY OUT OF THE MYSTERIOUS ETERNITY

'Damned impertinence!' I snapped. 'That's a classic quotation, not some jingle to be bandied around willy-nilly!'

'All very gimmicky,' agreed Gerard, 'and there's part of the quote missing as well.'

Just then Josephine sidled up to us.

'You two had better get yourselves moving,' she announced. 'The seats are going fast.'

'It's okay,' I replied. 'We've got complimentary seats reserved.'

'You're wrong there,' she said. 'They may be complimentary, but they're not reserved.'

I thought I detected a certain coolness in Josephine's tone of voice, as if Gerard and I were intruders at some exclusive gathering.

Apparently she'd forgotten that it was us who'd brought Macaulay along in the first place. Even so, we heeded her advice and made our way upstairs.

Not a moment too soon either! It seemed the event was a sell-out: the function room was packed to the gunwales. Fortunately, though, we had the advantage of distinguished friends: Hogarth and Swift were sitting in the back row with two empty chairs between them which they'd evidently 'reserved' for Gerard and me. We sat down gratefully and as we did I noticed Douglas observing us with derision from the doorway.

He glanced up at the clock, which now said 7.30, then stepped aside as Macaulay strode into the room. I was pleasantly surprised when the assembled throng broke into a hearty round of applause (there were also some whoops and whistles which I judged quite unnecessary) but the rumpus ceased once the great man started speaking.

'England is a naturally peaceful country,' he began, 'but under Henry the Eighth we acquired a reputation for bullying. By now the Welsh princes and Irish chieftains had been reduced to submission; yet successive kings of Scotland remained defiant. Henry wanted the infant Scottish princess Mary Stewart to be his future daughter-in-law. Rather than making peaceful overtures, however, he instead sent forces to ravage the borderlands. This 'rough wooing' (as it was known) only served to drive the Scots into a French alliance; and in due course the princess married the dauphin of France. She even Frenchified her name: for ever after she was known as Mary Stuart.'

Sitting in the front row were several women who were paying rapt attention to Macaulay's every word; and which he delivered in his usual manner: dignified, authoritative and concise.

'Needless to say,' he continued, 'the king himself was the worst bully of all. He bullied courtiers, he bullied ambassadors and he bullied Parliament. At his insistence, for example, the Parliament of 1533 declared that 'this realm of England is an empire'. The claim was clearly absurd, but at the time it suited Parliament to support Henry's ambitions. On other occasions the members argued with him, extracted concessions from him or simply pointed out flaws in his policy. This was their price for agreeing to his taxes. Often their words fell on deaf ears; periodically they were punished or expelled from the house; yet these ceaseless wrangles with the king served by degrees to make Parliament stronger, then indispensable, and eventually infallible.'

'Giving rise to a nice turn of phrase,' remarked Swift. "The infallibility of Parliament'.'

'But in whose opinion?' enquired Hogarth.

'Parliament's own opinion,' said Macaulay. 'Which in their view was all that really mattered.'

As the three of them conducted their brief debate they seemed oblivious to the fifty or so people who sat listening in awed silence; and once again it struck me that Macaulay, Hogarth and Swift occupied a different kind of world to the rest of us. They lived and breathed history, whereas we were merely interested observers. I noticed one or two individuals in the audience glance at one another knowingly as the early tussles between Monarch and Parliament were being discussed (tussles that would later lead to turmoil). Others, though, appeared utterly perplexed. Plainly some of this was going right over their heads, so I was pleased when Macaulay moved on to shipbuilding.

'To maintain the peace,' he announced, 'Henry the Eighth required an effective navy. Therefore fifty-three new warships were built which could discharge broadsides and blast foreign vessels clean out of the water. Such measures were believed to be essential. The king assumed that the whole of Europe was against him, which was more or less correct (the French and Spanish certainly were). The only exception was a confederation of German princes who were prepared to offer friendship if Henry would marry one of their sisters. The unfortunate princess chosen for this role was Anne of Cleves. She was required to travel from her home in Dusseldorf via Antwerp to Calais, then sail across to Kent and finally ride on horseback to Greenwich, but when she arrived she was flatly rejected by her new husband, who described her rather unkindly as 'the Flanders Mare'.'

Macaulay went on to inform us that the marriage was swiftly dissolved, thus signalling an end to the prospective German alliance. In terms of diplomacy it was an outright disaster. I happened to know that the Englishman who'd made all the arrangements lost his head as a direct consequence of this failure, yet not once did Macaulay refer to him (obviously the list of proscribed names still held sway). Instead he turned to Henry's later years, when the question of the succession became paramount.

'As long as the king lived,' he concluded, 'England endured an unhappy peace. Once he'd died, however, there was a deep foreboding.'

Throughout the talk, Douglas had been observing proceedings from the doorway, no doubt conducting a headcount whilst also assessing audience reaction. He had a proprietorial air about him which suggested he was fully in control of the event, therefore he looked rather surprised when Macaulay ceased speaking and swept past him and out of the room. If he'd been planning a question-and-answer session it was too late now: soon chairs were being hurriedly scraped back as Macaulay's horde of admirers set off in pursuit. Douglas had no choice but to follow them. In the meantime, Hogarth and Swift remained where they were, plainly immune to the call of the herd.

'Hadn't we better get downstairs?' said Gerard. 'Otherwise we might lose our favourite table.'

'Don't concern yourself,' replied Swift. 'Nobody else will sit there.'

Sure enough, when we finally descended to the bar we found the table quite empty apart from Macaulay, who sat alone waiting for his companions to join him. The crowd parted to allow Hogarth and Swift to pass by, but closed again before Gerard and I could get near.

'Never mind,' said Gerard. 'We've got to get some drinks anyway.'

He began working his way into the crush and I temporarily lost sight of him, which was when I realized I was standing behind Douglas. He'd been intercepted by a friend of his, the man who we'd seen buying a ticket the previous Monday; and who was seemingly a little disappointed.

'I was expecting a bit of domestic strife,' he said, 'but there was no mention of the other five wives.'

'No,' replied Douglas, 'I suppose there wasn't.'

'No lies, deceit and obfuscation.'

'Again no.'

'And definitely no chopping block.'

'Well, you needn't worry on that account,' said Douglas brightly. 'There'll be plenty of beheadings next week, and the week after.'

'Glad to hear it,' said his friend. 'A few timely executions should liven up the story.'

I quickly moved out of earshot and rejoined Gerard, who'd just succeeded in getting served at the bar.

'Remind me to tell you later,' I murmured. 'I've just overheard an interesting conversation.'

'Alright,' said Gerard. 'By the way, am I meant to be getting drinks for Macaulay, Hogarth and Swift?'

'I shouldn't bother,' I said. 'They're probably being taken care of.'

'But don't you owe Macaulay a pint?'

'Yes, but I'll keep that in reserve.'

'Okay.'

Gerard bought us a Guinness apiece, then with some difficulty we made our way to the table, where the three of them each sat with a full glass. Also present, inevitably, was Douglas (but not his friend). Once again he made a point of ignoring Gerard and me. Instead he directed a stream of questions at Macaulay concerning future talks.

'So we'll be moving onto Edward the Sixth next, will we?' he enquired.

'Probably not actually,' said Macaulay. 'He was a child king misdirected by adults.'

'But what about the Lord Protectors?'

'Their policies were disastrous; they debased the currency and introduced a threepenny coin worth tuppence.'

'Lady Jane Grey?'

'A luckless girl who was queen for a mere nine days. Hardly worth bothering about.'

'Mary Tudor?'

'Married the king of Spain against all advice. Threw England into grave danger.'

As these figures from history were summarily dismissed one after another, Douglas began to appear increasingly disconcerted. I had a fairly good idea which character he was leading up to, and I suspected he'd find the verdict most unsatisfactory. Perhaps he sensed this himself, because all of a sudden he stopped asking questions. Thereafter he sat gazing in silence at his glass of beer.

Gathered all around us, at the other tables, were Macaulay's new-found adherents, many wearing tailcoats with shiny buttons up the front. None of them chose to approach him in person; instead they seemed content to bask in his presence, occasionally casting glances in our direction or straining an ear to catch a word or two. For his part, Macaulay showed no sign of having even noticed them (although Hogarth undoubtedly did). So it was that we passed the rest of the evening under the close scrutiny of our neighbours, while at the same time enjoying complete isolation.

When the bell rang for last orders, Douglas headed for the bar, bought himself a drink and failed to return. I asked Macaulay, Hogarth and Swift if they'd like another but they politely declined my offer.

Soon they were heading for the door, the throng of loyal disciples parting as usual to let them through, and then they were gone.

Once I was sure we were alone, I told Gerard about the conversation I'd overheard.

'Douglas predicted several beheadings next week,' I said. 'He's plainly unaware of Macaulay's list.'

'Who do you think he meant?' enquired Gerard.

'Well, there's the two Lord Protectors, Somerset and Northumberland, then obviously Lady Jane Grey, her husband and her father, but we can assume they've already been ruled out.'

'Oh..... yes.'

'And later there's Mary Queen of Scots.'

'Was that Mary Stuart?'

'Correct.'

'Macaulay's already mentioned her. More than once in fact.'

'Yes,' I conceded, 'but only in passing. You know his aversion to all types of unpleasantness.'

'But she was a queen,' said Gerard, 'beheaded on English soil!'

'I know.'

'Surely she deserves more than a simple nod.'

'Maybe she does,' I said, 'but judging by past form I doubt if we'll hear any more of her.'

27.

I was coming to the conclusion that Macaulay's interpretation of history was less straightforward than it appeared. For a start, it was laden with contradictions. He was reluctant ever to portray England as an aggressor, yet he was the first to admit we'd gained a reputation for bullying. For this he apologized, while at the same time allowing Henry the Eighth to build fifty-three warships which could 'blast foreign vessels clean out of the water'. Apparently these were acceptable as long as the king didn't actually use them (which he didn't). Next there was the question of our conduct towards Wales, Ireland and Scotland, which was at best condescending and at worst downright shabby. Again Macaulay was repentant: clearly the people who dwelt in these lands of mountains, bogs and moors were entitled to live out their lives unmolested by outsiders. However, he would brook no criticism of our right to control the seas that surrounded them; to take all the best fish; and to leave only limpets and seaweed for the natives on the shore.

Similarly, it was quite reasonable for Drake and Hawkins to intercept Spanish treasure ships returning from the Americas, or to plunder Spanish carracks from the Spice Islands; but if the Spaniards came anywhere near the coast of England they were regarded as trespassers. Finally, of course, there was the peace itself (or rather the lack of it). Macaulay insisted again and again that England was a naturally peaceful country, yet from what I'd learnt our history was a perpetual series of disturbances brought on by violence, intrigue, jealousy and greed.

28.

'Who's been asking about muffled oars?' demanded Douglas.

A week had passed and he'd surprised us as we sat drinking quietly in the Royal Oak.

'Me,' I answered, 'if it's any of your business.'

'It certainly is my business,' he said. 'There's a very important episode approaching.'

'Oh yes?'

'Sunday the sixteenth of May 1568, to be precise. A daring escape in a fishing boat.'

Douglas had been standing over Gerard and me, but now that he had our full attention he sat down at the opposite side of the table.

'Shall I continue?' he asked.

'Please do,' I replied. 'We're all ears.'

'On that day a sovereign queen stole across the Solway to seek the assistance of another sovereign queen. She acted in good faith, yet for all her troubles she was locked in a castle and the keys thrown away.'

'It wasn't as bad as all that,' I remarked. 'She had servants waiting on her hand and foot.'

'She was a prisoner!' roared Douglas. 'For eighteen years!'

At the sound of his raised voice a hush fell over the entire pub. Several people standing at the bar turned around for a moment and peered in our direction. Douglas glared at them with defiance and one-by-one they turned away again. Very soon the general babble of conversation had resumed. Meanwhile he sat brooding in morose silence.

It seemed to me that Douglas had a highly romantic view of Mary Queen of Scots. What he'd told us was quite true, but he'd omitted to mention that her presence in England gravely imperilled the fragile peace which Queen Elizabeth had been trying to build after years of turbulence. The king of Spain wanted to put Mary on the English throne and she herself desired it. Accordingly she became involved in one conspiracy after another. The way she behaved she was more or less asking to have her head chopped off!

Even so, reigning monarchs were not supposed to execute other monarchs (especially their own cousins). It just wasn't done. They could defeat them in battle, imprison them for years, hold them for ransom or even make them row a barge along the river; but actually executing them was generally considered inadmissible. Elizabeth knew all this when she had Mary beheaded in 1587, and in subsequent years she was overcome with remorse.

Needless to say it was no use arguing these points with Douglas because he simply wouldn't listen. In his opinion Mary Queen of Scots had a viable claim to the crown of England (which was correct) and therefore her execution was a wrong which had to be righted. She was the head of the Stuart dynasty and could trace her ancestry right back as far as King Edgar the Peaceable. The trouble was, so could Elizabeth the First; and so could Lady Catherine Grey; and so could King Philip of Spain; and a few others too. That was the reality. As things stood, most of England supported Elizabeth Tudor (most but not all) and the folly of the Stuarts was yet to be revealed.

In the meantime, another momentous event was about to unfold.

29.

'England is a naturally peaceful country,' said Macaulay, 'yet when a huge Armada appeared in the Channel plainly something had to be done. Obviously we'd guessed they were coming (the threat had been on the cards for years) but the Spaniards tried the usual foreigners' trick of arriving on a Saturday. They hoped to slip past Plymouth before anybody noticed, and were unaware that Admiral Howard was waiting in the harbour. As soon as they'd gone by he put to sea with his doughty English ships; then he harried the Spanish fleet for a week as it sailed gradually eastward.'

Macaulay went on to explain that the Spanish Armada was meant to link up with a vast army already stationed on the coast of Flanders; then escort it across the Channel and invade England.

'Unfortunately for the Spaniards,' he continued, 'there was nowhere safe for a large fleet to anchor once they'd passed the Isle Of Wight. In consequence the invasion plans were doomed.'

The story of how the Armada was driven off had Macaulay's audience on the edge of their seats. Squadrons of fighting ships led by Howard, Drake, Hawkins, Frobisher and Seymour attacked again and again, then fireships were sent in to cause panic amongst the Spanish seamen, finally a great storm blew up and scattered the Armada in the North Sea.

'The danger had been averted,' said Macaulay, 'and naturally it was Queen Elizabeth who took all the credit. It should be added, however, that she hardly contributed a penny towards the campaign. Moreover, she insisted that her navy was manned by privateers and should therefore be self-financing; because of this, many soldiers and sailors went home without any wages. It was typical of the way she handled affairs: Elizabeth was actually a very slippery individual. There are countless examples. Her rallying speech to the troops at Tilbury is well-known, but as a matter of fact she delayed its delivery until she was quite certain the Armada had been dispersed.'

Macaulay paused and gave a sigh.

'Just like her father,' he said, 'Elizabeth kept England isolated from the rest of Europe for many years, even refusing to accept the new-style Gregorian calendar which was widely accepted throughout the continent. As a result, we remained ten days behind everybody else; hence a reputation for awkwardness was added to the growing list of our perceived national failings. Furthermore, Elizabeth confused foreign envoys by always referring to herself as a king (which she clearly wasn't), addressing them in different languages (she understood many), and flirting with suitors she had no intention of marrying.'

From my vantage point in the back row of the function room I listened with interest as Macaulay set forth his critique of Elizabeth the First. It struck me that the way he dealt with her was no less harsh than the treatment he'd meted out to the Normans, the Plantagenets and the early Tudors: evidently he was no fan of Elizabeth's either.

Beside me sat Hogarth and Swift, both of whom I noticed had been rather quiet lately; and watching from the doorway was Douglas. His face had betrayed mild astonishment when Macaulay by-passed the imprisonment and execution of Mary Queen of Scots (just as I'd predicted) and instead moved directly onto the Spanish Armada. The lack of any other reaction suggested that Douglas was in awe of Macaulay and therefore reluctant to speak out (unless, of course, he was a very cool customer simply biding his time; it was hard to tell). As I sat pondering all this I suddenly realized Macaulay had ceased talking. He peered at his audience for a few moments.

'So,' he said at length, 'what was the real reason for the defeat of the Spanish Armada?'

It was a good question. In the past hour or so we'd heard how the Spaniards had started with a hundred and forty ships against a meagre force of only thirty-four, which implied that the English must have out-witted them, out-sailed them and out-gunned them. In the background, though, lurked an undeniable fact, namely, the unseasonal storm that drove the Armada around the coast of Scotland and onto the rocks of Ireland. An expectant silence descended over the room as we awaited Macaulay's judgement.

'No doubt there were many heroics,' he declared at last, 'but actually it was the weather that saved us.'

Without a further word, Macaulay swept through the doorway and out of the room, pursued down the staircase by the majority of the crowd (including Douglas and Gerard, obviously eager to get a beer).

I stood up to follow after them, only to feel a restraining hand on my sleeve. Looking around, I discovered that Hogarth and Swift were still in their seats and gesturing for me to sit down again.

'Can we have a discreet word before you go?' said Swift.

'Sure,' I answered. 'Nothing wrong, is there?'

'Hopefully not,' he said, 'but we were wondering if you knew about Macaulay's list?'

'Well, I've got an inkling, yes.'

'So you understand the problem that lies ahead?'

'I think so.'

Swift nodded, then conferred briefly with Hogarth before turning to me once more.

'The trouble is,' he continued, 'we're a little concerned about our mutual friend.'

'You mean Douglas?'

'Yes,' said Swift. 'Jacobite, is he?'

'Well, he is when it suits him,' I replied. 'He lives in England and pays taxes in England, but his accent varies depending on who he's talking to.'

'Oh yes,' said Hogarth, 'we know that type.'

'But I'm certain he's quite harmless.'

They conferred again.

'Do you think he's aware of the list?' enquired Swift.

'I think it's beginning to dawn on him, yes.'

'We thought so.'

'We're worried he might interfere with the peace,' added Hogarth.

'The peace according to Macaulay?'

'Quite.'

'It's difficult to tell,' I said. 'He's obviously looking forward to the Stuart century.'

'Then he's bound to be disappointed,' Swift pronounced, 'whichever way the axe falls.'

After further discussion the three of us decided that all we could do was continue to observe Douglas and hope for a satisfactory outcome. If he was indeed aware of the list, then surely he would realize that self-restraint was imperative. After all, we told ourselves, he was still nominally hosting the 'peace talks' and therefore it stood to reason that any kind of disruption was against his interests.

The thought never occurred to us that we might face interference from other quarters.

30.

'What's all this about a list?' said Josephine.

It was the following evening, and I was meeting Gerard for an early pint. Josephine was behind the bar, but refused to serve me until I'd answered her question.

'It's not my list,' I replied. 'It's Macaulay's.'

'So?'

'Well, can't you ask him?'

'I'm asking you!' she snapped. 'Is there a list or is there not?'

I realized I had no choice but to surrender.

'Yes, there is,' I said. 'It's a list of people who were executed, murdered or killed in battle on English soil.'

'And Macaulay misses them all out, does he?'

'Mostly, yes, although one or two have slipped through the net. He once referred to Harold Godwinson, for example; and he also mentioned Richard the Third.'

Josephine eyed me sternly.

'Don't try and bamboozle me,' she said. 'As a rule he misses most of them out.'

'Yes.'

She shook her head. 'No wonder revenues have fallen recently.'

'Oh, sorry,' I said. 'I had no idea.'

'There was a slight recovery for the Spanish Armada, but the overall trend is downward; and now I know why: it's not peace and tranquillity that sells beer, it's violence, intrigue, jealousy and greed.'

It transpired that Josephine had been approached directly by the man who always sat in the front row at Macaulay's talks; the same man who'd bemoaned the lack of beheadings. Apparently his name was Herbert; and it seemed that he, too, had guessed the existence of the list. Now he'd gone and informed Josephine, which meant the secret was out.

In due course she served up a couple of drinks, but she hadn't finished with me yet.

'The question now,' she announced, 'is what are you going to do about it?'

'Me?' I said with astonishment. 'What can I do?'

Josephine gave me an icy smile.

'Oh,' she said, 'I'm sure you'll think of something.'

I retreated to our usual table, where Gerard was waiting anxiously. It took me a minute or two before I recovered from the shock; then I explained the situation to him.

'It's not fair,' I said. 'It should be Douglas sorting all this out, not me.'

'Agreed,' said Gerard, 'but the fact is, Douglas doesn't take orders from anyone.'

'And I do?'

'Yes.'

'Oh.....right.'

'Besides which, you're closer to Macaulay than anybody else.

Don't forget he let you have his pint of Guinness when you were desperate.'

'That wasn't much of a sacrifice!' I protested. 'He didn't want it anyway!'

'Doesn't matter,' said Gerard. 'It's the thought that counts.'

He was correct, of course, so I gave up arguing and instead searched for a solution.

'Well,' I said, 'I can hardly persuade Macaulay to abandon the list. It would upset his hypothesis of England at peace.'

'It doesn't have to be abandoned altogether,' replied Gerard, 'just diluted slightly.'

'Suppose so.'

'That should keep Josephine satisfied.'

'Possibly.'

Gerard pondered for a moment or two.

'So who's next on the list?'

'Guy Fawkes.'

'Then it's easy!' he exclaimed in triumph. 'Macaulay can't possibly miss him out!'

I wasn't so sure.

31.

Next day, Gerard and I returned to the Portrait Gallery and wandered through the section labelled 'Stuarts'.

We paused to examine a picture of King James the First, the story of whose accession was well-known. In March 1603 a lone horseman rode from London to Edinburgh to inform James that Queen Elizabeth was dead; and that she'd named him as her successor. Within days he abandoned Scotland, never to return, and headed south to claim his inheritance.

'Ironic really,' I said. 'A Scottish king took the crown of England; yet it's the Scots who've been clamouring for independence ever since.'

'It ought to be the other way around,' remarked Gerard.

'Indeed.'

As a matter of fact, the reign of King James passed in relative peace; and was marred only by the Gunpowder Plot.

Unsurprisingly, there were no pictures of Guy Fawkes. He'd been living incognito before he was caught attempting to blow up King and Parliament and he didn't survive for very long after that. As a consequence, nobody bothered painting his portrait.

What was on display, however, was a copy of a signed confession extracted under torture from Guido Fawkes (which was his proper name). The signature was virtually indecipherable. Nearby hung an explanatory notice.

'It says here,' announced Gerard, 'that the king gave specific instructions for only the gentler tortures to be used.'

'Really?'

'That doesn't sound too bad, does it?'

I gave Gerard a penetrating look.

'If I were you,' I said, 'I should read on.'

He obeyed my command and continued to read in silence. I watched as his eyes moved further down the notice; then suddenly he drew a deep breath and winced.

'Ooh, no,' he said at length. 'I see what you mean. Hardly a nice ending.'

'Quite.'

'Definitely a candidate for Macaulay's list.'

'Yes.'

'So presumably there'll be no mention of the Gunpowder Plot?'

'I doubt it.'

We decided to move on.

The Stuart kings had seemingly been portrayed by all the leading artists of their day. They gazed out at us from their gilded frames and without exception they appeared vain, egotistical and supercilious.

The most vain, egotistical and supercilious by far, of course, was King Charles the First. In one particularly huge canvas he was depicted in left profile, right profile and looking straight ahead.

'There he is,' I said. 'The man at the heart of our problem.'

'Surely it's Macaulay's problem, not ours,' observed Gerard. 'After all, he's a bona fide historian while we're only amateurs.'

'I don't think it's that simple,' I replied. 'We've all been aware of the list for quite some time: Swift, Hogarth, you, me, Douglas and now even Herbert. A few of us harboured reservations yet failed to speak out, blithely assuming that Macaulay would find a way around the problem.'

'Well, perhaps he will.'

'How can he though?' I demanded. 'It's a list of people killed in battle, murdered or executed on English soil. How can he not include a king who was publicly beheaded in London?'

Gerard shrugged.

'Don't know.'

We sat down on a bench opposite a picture of Oliver Cromwell.

'Actually,' I said, 'we've jumped forward rather quickly. Charles wasn't just executed out of the blue; there were all sorts of goings-on before that: the king's refusal to recognize parliamentary privilege; his preference for court favourites; his interference with free trade; his illegal taxes; uproar in the House of Commons; eleven years' rule without parliament; royal demands for ship money; parliament recalled and dissolved again; riots in London; a Scottish invasion; another parliament; MP's threatened with arrest; more riots and finally civil war. They all played a part in the king's demise.'

'Good grief,' said Gerard. 'Scarcely any peace and tranquillity there.'

'No,' I agreed, 'just a profusion of violence, intrigue, jealousy and greed.'

'But will it be enough to placate Josephine?'

'You might well ask.'

We spent another half hour drifting past portraits of the later Stuarts (no less vain, egotistical and supercilious than their predecessors) and then we went home. We'd reached the conclusion there was little we could do except await developments at the next talk, which was scheduled for the following Wednesday.

By then, however, Josephine had taken matters into her own hands.

32.

THE ROYAL OAK

PRESENTS

'ENGLAND IN TURMOIL'

A TALK BY

THOMAS BABINGTON MACAULAY

FEATURING

THE TRIAL AND EXECUTION OF

KING CHARLES THE FIRST

WEDNESDAY AT 7.30 PM

TICKETS £5

BOOK NOW

'She must have been reading ahead,' I remarked, as we stood peering at the new poster.

'Unless she's been consulting with Macaulay,' suggested Gerard.

'Hardly likely,' I said. 'Not his style at all.'

'No, I suppose you're right.'

'He probably doesn't know anything about it.'

It was seven o'clock on Wednesday evening, and we'd just spotted the poster pinned to the notice-board at the foot of the staircase. A few people were already starting to make their way up to the function room. Josephine had apparently delegated Terence to take care of ticket sales; he was seated at the table and chair formerly occupied by Douglas.

'Come on,' I said. 'We'd better go and see whether Macaulay and the others have turned up yet.'

We went through to the bar and glanced around, but there was no sign of them.

'Guinness?' enquired Gerard.

'Yes, please,' I said.

As Gerard worked his way through the gathering throng I sat down in our usual corner and reflected on the state of play. Evidently, Douglas had been knocked off his perch and doubtless his feathers would be temporarily ruffled. Even so, there was no question of him failing to attend this evening's talk; after all, it presented him with a whole array of new opportunities. The so-called 'martyrdom' of Charles the First was merely the beginning of a series of catastrophes which beset the Stuart dynasty; and as a loyal sympathiser Douglas was now at liberty to wallow in the injustice of their downfall. I could just imagine the fuss he was bound to make at every twist and turn of the tale; which meant, of course, that he'd be more insufferable than ever.

Meanwhile, we still had to face the dilemma of Macaulay's list. I had no idea what Josephine was expecting, but I sensed it was a 'make-or-break' evening; and when Gerard returned with the drinks my misgivings were confirmed. He sat down looking quite shaken.

'Josephine's just given me a grilling,' he said. 'She wanted to know why Macaulay wasn't here yet; whether we'd seen the contents of tonight's talk; and did we have an advance copy?'

'What did you tell her?'

'Well, I pointed out that Macaulay never uses notes and always delivers his talks from the top of his head.'

'Good.'

'And I promised her he'd be here presently.'

'Let's hope your right.'

The clock now said twenty past seven. Macaulay was cutting it a bit fine, but I told myself that was his prerogative. He'd never been late before and I was certain he would arrive in good time.

'There are plenty of people heading for the function room,' said Gerard, 'so that should keep Josephine off our backs for the time being.'

We watched as Douglas emerged from the crowd at the far end of the bar, deliberately ignored us, and marched straight upstairs without paying. Terence made no attempt to stop him, but when we decided to follow he insisted we part with five pounds each.

'Actually, we're entitled to complimentary tickets,' I explained.

Terence raised his eyebrows.

'Sorry,' he said. 'I've been told nothing about that.'

'You can ask Josephine.'

'No, I can't,' he replied. 'You can.'

After a hurried debate, Gerard and agreed that it would be easier simply to pay up, so we forked out the money and went upstairs. The function room was almost full, but luckily we managed to find somewhere to sit. Nearby a couple of chairs had been reserved for Hogarth and Swift; their arrival a few minutes later caused the usual stir: it meant that Macaulay was now in the building.

At least, I assumed he was.

I signalled for the two of them to join us and they came over. They both looked rather flustered.

'Everything alright?' I asked.

'More or less,' murmured Swift, 'but Macaulay is furious about that damned silly notice downstairs.'

'Ah?'

'Not your work, I shouldn't think?'

'No, fortunately.'

There wasn't time for further discussion because it was now precisely seven thirty. Hogarth and Swift reached their chairs and sat down just as Macaulay came sweeping through the doorway. He strode to the front of the room, then turned to address his audience.

'Somebody once asked,' he began, 'what lessons could be learnt from history.
There were others who scoffed at this question (people who should have known better) but I can assure you there are indeed many lessons.'

From where I was sitting I could see Herbert in his usual place in the front row. He was the man who'd made the original enquiry all those weeks ago; and I thought I saw him nod his head in acknowledgement. The identity of the 'scoffers' wasn't clear; but I guessed I was included amongst the suspects. For a few moments I felt like a pupil who'd been called into the headmaster's study. To my relief, however, Macaulay took the matter no further.

'We learnt from King Edgar,' he continued, 'that people in boats need to cooperate if they're going to get anywhere; the same applies to ships; and it's a lesson that's held sway ever since England had a navy. Then the Vikings came along and taught us how to sail better than anybody else. Canute taught us that the powers of a king are limited. William the Conqueror instilled in Englishmen the desire to own property; he also taught us that possession is nine-tenths of the law.'

Over to my left I observed Douglas taking his notebook and pencil from his pocket. Soon he was furiously scribbling these words of wisdom. Macaulay was now in full flow.

'From Magna Carta we learnt always to keep copies of important documents, the Plantagenets taught us not to interfere in neighbouring countries (a lesson, of course, which has never been heeded); the Tudors taught us to regard all foreign ships as pirates and blast them clean out of the water. Finally, we learnt from the Stuarts that the monarchy will never go away because there's always somebody, somewhere, with a claim to the throne.'

Macaulay paused and glanced around him.

'Shall I go on?' he asked.

'Please do,' said Douglas. 'We're all ears.'

He had now ceased writing and was staring without expression at his notebook.

It was impossible to tell what he was thinking.

'England is a naturally peaceful country,' declared Macaulay, 'but the Stuarts endangered the peace with their selfishness, their double-dealing and their pride. The indictments against them are numerous: James the First was handed the crown of England on a plate but showed the ingratitude of a spoilt child; Charles the First declared war on his own subjects and was dealt with accordingly; Charles the Second helped extinguish the Great Fire of London but did little else worthy of merit; and James the Second repeatedly flouted the will of parliament.'

All of a sudden, Macaulay fixed his gaze on me.

'And so at last,' he said, 'we come to a tale of muffled oars.'

Three or four people in the audience peered in my direction, as though I was somehow 'in' with Macaulay. I knew for a fact that I wasn't; nonetheless I allowed myself to bask in reflected glory for a moment or two. Meanwhile, he resumed his account.

'In December 1688, London was in uproar. Only when it was too late, James the Second realized his luck had run out. In the dead of night he escaped in a rowing boat with muffled oars, travelled down the River Thames, and fled into exile in France.'

Macaulay went on to explain that James had left the throne unoccupied, which Parliament then used as an excuse to offer it to William of Orange, who'd conveniently landed at Torbay a few weeks earlier. Soon the new King William was firmly established in London. James was left marooned in Europe, roaming from one royal court to the next, and spent the rest of his life planning someday to return to England and rule once more.

'His descendants,' Macaulay concluded, 'were known as the 'kings over the water'.'

With that he turned and headed for the doorway, accompanied by a tumultuous round of applause, and was followed down the staircase by the usual horde of devotees. Needless to say, Josephine was delighted; the bar filled up quickly and the drink began to flow.

Yet when Gerard and I went downstairs to join in with the fun and jollity, we noticed that somebody had made themselves absent.

Douglas, it transpired, had stormed out of the door without saying goodnight to anyone.

33.

'Who's next on the list?' enquired Gerard.

'Not sure really,' I replied. 'There were far fewer conspiracies, murders or executions once William was installed as king; neither were there any more battles; not in this country at least.'

Gerard examined his glass of beer thoughtfully.

'So where did this William pop up from?'

'He was Dutch actually,' I said, 'but he had quite a lot going for him: he could trace his ancestry as far back as Edgar the Peaceable; his wife was an English princess; and furthermore he recognized the rights of Parliament.'

'So everybody was happy.'

'Correct.'

We drank our beers.

Gerard and I were in a mood of cautious optimism. Josephine had just informed us that we could take charge of the 'peace talks', as she called them, because Douglas had gone missing. Apparently there'd been no sign of him since the evening of Macaulay's triumph.

'He left here in a terrific huff,' she announced.

It so happened I knew the precise reason for his disgruntlement, but when I began recounting the details to Josephine she quickly lost patience.

'Alright, that's enough,' she said, abruptly cutting me off. 'Just get the next talk organized, will you? I'm much too busy.'

After she'd left us we went through to have a look at the notice board. The offending poster from the previous week was still there. It said: 'ENGLAND IN TURMOIL'. Carefully we took it down and folded it away; then, when we'd made sure Josephine definitely wasn't coming back, we replaced it with a new one. The message was simple: **'ENGLAND AT PEACE'**.

34.

CONSIDER HISTORY, WITH THE BEGINNINGS OF IT STRETCHING DIMLY INTO THE REMOTE TIME, EMERGING DARKLY OUT OF THE MYSTERIOUS ETERNITY: THE TRUE EPIC POEM AND DIVINE UNIVERSAL SCRIPTURE.

Macaulay's room was the same as ever; there was the classic inscription on the wall above the fireplace; the bottle of port on the dresser; and the row of pegs where Macaulay, Hogarth and Swift had hung their tailcoats with shiny buttons up the front. A fire was crackling in the hearth, although outside it was a warm spring day, and the three of them were lounging in their armchairs.

Today, however, they weren't 'considering history' so much as discussing national character.

'I'm the first to confess,' said Macaulay, 'that the English people are not without fault. We've been accused of insularity and awkwardness, and we've been called bullies.'

'Drunkards,' added Hogarth.

'Hypocrites,' said Swift.

'Yes, well, possibly,' conceded Macaulay. 'We also have a tendency to decide what's best for other people. So it was that when the English Parliament chose William of Orange, they chose him to reign not only over England, but also Scotland, Wales and Ireland; and, of course, they did this without consulting the natives. The same applied later when they crowned the pliable and obedient Queen Anne as William's successor, and later still with King George the First, who was actually a German nobleman who spoke no English (a fact that suited Parliament very well indeed). Such decisions were taken on the assumption that what was best for England was best for everyone else too.'

Macaulay went on to outline the slightly dubious machinations by which Parliament achieved supremacy; and he admitted that it would be fair to add the charge of high-handedness to the list of our national shortcomings.

'Mind you,' he continued, 'these faults were minor compared with those of Lewis.'

'Oh, yes, Lewis,' I said casually. 'I'd forgotten all about him.'

Macaulay, Hogarth and Swift all stared at me in disbelief.

'Forgotten about Lewis?' uttered Hogarth. 'How could you forget a man who was the scourge of Europe for decades?'

'My apologies,' I said, 'but I didn't know he had anything to do with England at peace.'

'On the contrary,' said Macaulay. 'He had everything to do with it. You'll recall when I explained the theory that peace brings prosperity, which in turn leads to pride, which then leads to confrontation?'

'Yes,' I answered. 'I remember.'

'Well, Lewis was the personification of pride, while England remained a few steps behind still struggling for prosperity. We had no wish for outright confrontation, but when he disrupted our foreign trade we began gradually to be drawn into his wars.'

'In other words,' said Swift, 'to preserve peace in England we went and fought overseas.'

'Correct,' said Macaulay, 'and it's a sobering thought that these campaigns were largely financed by a tax on beer.'

'Outrageous,' remarked Gerard.

'The cause of many a riot,' said Hogarth.

Gerard and I had only dropped in at Macaulay's room to check the arrangements for the next talk, but now we found ourselves appraising international affairs in the early eighteenth century.

'It wasn't just the French who disrupted our trade,' resumed Macaulay. 'The Spanish were equally guilty; which was the reason why we fought the War of Jenkin's Ear.'

Gerard smiled broadly.

'Sounds rather quaint,' he said. "The War of Jenkin's Ear'. What was that all about then?'

'I'd prefer not to go into the details,' came the reply. 'Suffice to say it wasn't very pleasant.'

The smile faded as realization dawned.

'You mean for Jenkins?' said Gerard.

'I'm afraid so.'

'I see.'

By now the smile had vanished completely. Gerard touched his own ear distractedly, as if to reassure himself it was still there, but he asked no further questions.

There was a lull in the conversation, so I took the opportunity to make an enquiry of my own.

'I was just wondering,' I said, 'will we still be talking about 'England at Peace' after 1707?'

'Of course,' said Macaulay.

'But I thought it changed to 'Great Britain'.'

'Aha,' he said. 'I see what you're driving at. Let's just say as a general rule that 'England' and 'Great Britain' are mutually transposable, depending on the circumstances. If we wish to assert ourselves, for instance, we allude to 'British Sea Power'; on the other hand, when we want to express our peaceful intentions, we find that 'England' has a more agreeable ring to it.'

'What about 'The United Kingdom'?' said Gerard.

Macaulay gave him an indulgent look.

'Well, yes,' he said, 'some people insist on using that term, but I tend not to bother.'

'Oh.'

'Rather uninspiring, don't you think?'

'Suppose.'

'And, besides, we all know what we mean by 'England'.'

'Not always peaceful though,' remarked Hogarth. 'You should have seen London during the South Sea Bubble. Hardly a picture of tranquillity.'

'A regrettable episode,' said Macaulay. 'Nevertheless, lessons were learnt and the underlying peace remained intact.'

'Peace or no peace!' snapped Swift. 'It was an unalloyed swindle!'

'The national debt sold off to speculators,' added Hogarth. 'I remember there was a public outcry: 'Somebody should be sent to the Tower!''

'Somebody was,' said Macaulay. 'The Chancellor of the Exchequer, to be precise.'

'That didn't solve the crisis,' said Swift.

'No,' said Macaulay. 'The crisis was solved by the Bank of England: it covered the debt, established a sinking fund and created a gold reserve. With these safeguards in place the financial panic subsided, prosperity returned and the peace remained intact. In due course the Bank became invincible.'

As the discussion went on, I was once again impressed by the way Macaulay always stuck to his guns as far as peace was concerned. In the past few minutes there'd been a slight suggestion of dissent from Hogarth and Swift, but I interpreted this as a healthy example of free speech in action. Parliament would have been proud of them.

A little later, Gerard and I made our excuses and departed, having fixed the next talk for the following Wednesday. We intended to head directly home, but when we emerged into the evening sunlight we decided to go for a stroll through the park first. We wandered towards the ornamental lake, and after a while I became aware that Gerard had fallen silent. He was evidently deep in thought.

'Did you notice,' he said at length, 'how knowledgeable. Hogarth and Swift seemed about the period?'

'Yes,' I replied, 'I did notice.'

'It was almost as though they were caught up in the South Sea Bubble themselves.'

'Well, a lot of people were.'

Gerard furrowed his brow.

'And this 'sinking fund' that Macaulay mentioned. Was it to do with ships?'

'No,' I said. 'It was to do with money.'

'So they put money in and it disappeared without trace?'

'I think it was the other way around actually,' I ventured. 'Macaulay said it was a safeguard.'

'How did it work then?'

'Don't know.'

By the time we'd completed a circuit of the lake we'd reached the conclusion that we had no choice but to return to Macaulay's room and ask him to explain about the sinking fund.

'Presumably they'll all still be there,' said Gerard.

His prediction was correct. As we approached along the corridor we could clearly hear Hogarth speaking. It sounded as if he was reading from a list, so I signalled to Gerard to wait for a moment.

'The Massacre of Glencoe?' said Hogarth.

'No,' replied Macaulay.

'The Porteous Affair?'

'No.'

'The Canter of Coltbridge?'

'No.'

'Prestonpans?'

'No.'

'Culloden?'

'No.'

There was a pause.

'Culloden?' said Swift. 'I don't remember that.'

'No, you wouldn't,' said Macaulay. 'It was after your time.'

'Ah, yes.'

Another pause.

'Shall I continue?' said Hogarth.

'Please do,' said Swift. 'We're all ears.'

'The Suppression of the Clans?'

'No,' said Macaulay.

'The Prohibition of the Kilt and Tartan?'

'No.'

I turned to Gerard, put my finger to my lips, and the two of us retreated quietly back along the corridor.

'Aren't we going to ask about the sinking fund?' he enquired, when we got outside.

'Probably not,' I answered. 'I think we'd better leave it for the time being.'

35.

That night I lay in bed pondering the conversation we'd overheard. It reminded me of a similar exchange between the three of them several weeks earlier, and gave me a rather queasy feeling.

Next morning I suggested to Gerard that we pay another visit to the Portrait Gallery.

'Any particular reason?' he asked.

'No, no,' I replied, 'but I thought it might be helpful to match some names with faces.'

'You mean the next batch of kings and queens?'

'Er...yes...and maybe one or two other people as well.'

'Righto.'

So it was that we arrived at the gallery and once more passed through the section labelled 'STUARTS'. At the far end hung pictures of James the Second, his daughters Mary and Anne, and finally Mary's husband William of Orange.

At this point the gallery divided into several rooms. Straight ahead was the main room labelled 'HANOVERIANS. On the right was a room dedicated to the Jacobites and their adherents; and on the left was an annexe with a sign reading 'ARTS AND HUMANITIES'. I ushered Gerard into the Jacobites room and left him peering at the many flattering portraits of Bonnie Prince Charlie. Meanwhile, I slipped briefly away to 'ARTS AND HUMANITIES'.

Here were displayed poets, painters, illustrators, sculptors, satirists, playwrights, actors, actresses, essayists, composers, chroniclers and diarists. Each picture was accompanied by an explanatory notice giving their date of birth and death. I cast my eyes over them and soon found the ones I was looking for. A quick glance told me all I needed to know; then I went back and rejoined Gerard.

'See anything interesting?' he asked.

'Yes,' I replied. 'Very interesting indeed.'

36.

'England is a naturally peaceful country,' said Macaulay, 'but when Highland warriors appeared in Derbyshire plainly something needed to be done. They were led by the so-called 'Young Pretender', Charles Edward Stuart, and behind them they'd left a trail of disruption.'

As Macaulay delivered his talk, I gazed around at my fellow listeners. The function room was reasonably full, I thought, and the audience was attentive. What was slightly disconcerting, however, was the complete absence of Hogarth and Swift.

When Macaulay had arrived at seven twenty-five he'd come alone. He'd offered no explanation as I accompanied him upstairs, and because the talk was due to begin at any minute I hadn't pursued the matter. All the same, the gathering seemed somehow different without the two stalwarts. Herbert was sitting in the front row as normal, while Gerard and I occupied the rear.

There were several other regulars and a few newcomers: hopefully a turnout good enough to satisfy Josephine.

'The 'Young Pretender' was leading his people into disaster,' continued Macaulay. 'He expected to be made welcome in London on behalf of the exiled James the Third, but gradually his support dwindled and finally he decided to retreat back to Scotland. The task of chasing him away was given to the Duke of Cumberland, who successfully brought the rising to an end. In consequence, the peace remained intact.'

At this stage I saw Herbert remove a notebook and pencil from his pocket and begin making notes, just as Douglas had on previous occasions. I wouldn't have been surprised if he was planning to report back to Douglas: the pair were obviously colluding with one another. Still, it was none of my business, so I decided to pay no further attention to Herbert.

Macaulay went on to describe how England gradually recovered from the shock of being invaded; how the French had undoubtedly encouraged the 'Young Pretender'; and how soon afterwards our maritime trade started improving by leaps and bounds.

'The navy was no longer tied down in defence of our coast,' he concluded, 'and was now free to command the wider oceans.'

In his customary fashion Macaulay turned and headed for the doorway, accompanied by rapturous applause. Gerard and I joined the multitude that followed in his wake, but when we finally got downstairs we found him sitting alone at the usual table. Fortunately, his admirers were keeping their distance.

'Pint of Guinness?' I enquired.

'Thank you, yes,' he said.

I gave Gerard some money and he went off to get the drinks. Meanwhile, I sat down beside Macaulay. I was suddenly very conscious that the queasy feeling had returned.

A long moment passed.

'Interesting talk,' I said. 'The demise of the Jacobites.'

'More or less,' answered Macaulay, 'though their descendants are most likely still out there somewhere, watching and waiting.'

'Yes.'

I glanced towards the bar, where Gerard was busy placing our order; then I took a deep breath, turned to Macaulay, and asked the question I'd been avoiding all evening.

'What's become of Hogarth and Swift?'

'I'm afraid they've had to bow out,' came the reply.

'Ah,'

'The constraints of time, you understand?'

'I think so, yes.'

'Good.'

Macaulay gave me a discreet nod, and at that moment I realized the matter was now closed. Just then Gerard returned clutching three pints of Guinness, which he set down on the table before us.

'So,' he said breezily, 'what's become of Hogarth and Swift?'

'I'll explain later,' I said. 'Let's drink a toast in their absence, shall we? Cheers!'

The three of us raised our glasses, and as we drank I casually wondered if any of the bystanders had been eavesdropping. The crowd was slowly beginning to disperse, but several of them had been peering in our direction for the past few minutes. They couldn't have helped noticing that Hogarth and Swift were no longer present. Whether anybody had guessed the reason why, however, was difficult to tell. Thankfully, the queasy feeling had started to subside. Even so, I was quite relieved when Macaulay changed the subject.

'By the way,' he said, 'I was hoping the two of you could drop in at my room tomorrow?'

'Of course,' I replied.

'There's something I'd like you to help me with.'

37.

We arrived at ten o'clock the following morning and discovered Macaulay sitting quietly in his usual armchair examining a sheaf of papers. He was so absorbed with his studies that for a few seconds he failed to notice us standing in the doorway. Eventually, I gave a gentle knock and he looked up.

'Ah, good, you're here,' he said. 'Help yourselves to a glass of port.'

'It's rather early,' I remarked, but Gerard had already gone over to the dresser and was soon pouring out three glasses. After he'd handed them around we sat down opposite the fire, which was smouldering gently.

'Now what I'd like one of you to do,' said Macaulay, 'is read aloud from this list.' He indicated the papers in his hand. 'So who's going to volunteer?'

'Me,' said Gerard.

I had no objection, so he reached over and took the papers from Macaulay, who now issued a series of instructions.

'Start reading from the top of the second page,' he said. 'Employ an interrogatory style; then pause briefly after each item to allow me to give an answer.'

'Right,' said Gerard. 'Got that.'

'Begin when you're ready.'

There was a short delay while Gerard cleared his throat, and then at last he began.

'The Trial of Admiral Byng.'

'Interrogatory, please,' said Macaulay.

'Oh, yes, sorry,' said Gerard. 'The Trial of Admiral Byng?'

'No,' came the reply.

'The Stamp Act?'

'No.'

'The Excise on Tea?'

'No.'

'Lexington?'

'No.'

'Bunker Hill?'

'No.'

'The Imprisonment of Wilkes?'

'No.'

'The Gordon Riots?'

'No.'

'The Laws of Seditious Libel?'

'No.'

'The Surrender at Yorktown?'

'No.'

Gerard continued reading from the list, and at some stage I happened to glance across at Macaulay. He was reclining in his armchair with his eyes closed, answering each question as if responding to some mystical litany. The reply was invariably 'no', and he appeared to be going through a predetermined ritual rather than making any kind of judgement. Moreover, I got the strong impression he knew the contents of the list by heart: no doubt he'd heard it many times before.

Gradually, I began to realise there was a common element running through the list.

'The Rotten Boroughs?' said Gerard.

'No,' said Macaulay.

'The Workhouses?'

'No.'

'The Corn Laws?'

'No.'

'The Press Gangs?'

'No.'

'The Suspension of Habeas Corpus?'

'No.'

'The Naval Mutiny?'

'No.'

'The Bombardment of Copenhagen?'

'No.

'The Highland Clearances?'

'No.'

'The Acts of Enclosure?'

'No.

'The Irish Potato Famine?'

'No.'

And so it went on.

After a while, Macaulay waved his hand and signalled Gerard to cease. He then reached over and retrieved the sheaf of papers, which he laid carefully to one side.

'Thank you,' he remarked in a weary tone. 'That's got that over and done with.'

A little later, Gerard and I were dismissed from Macaulay's presence. He thanked us once again for our trouble, and said he hoped to see us at the next talk, which was scheduled for the following Wednesday.

Once we'd emerged into the daylight, Gerard turned to me and asked the meaning of the list.

'Well, as far as I can tell,' I said, 'it's a list of episodes in which England doesn't appear in a particularly good light.'

'Oh,' said Gerard. 'I see.'

'We overheard Hogarth reading from it the other week, if you remember: the Suppression of the Clans, the Prohibition of the Tartan and so forth. They're events and situations we're not very proud of as a nation.'

'So why does Macaulay insist on hearing them all?'

'I think he regards the list as a kind of purge which he puts himself through in order to absolve the rest of us.'

'Blimey.'

'He wants nothing to obstruct his vision of England at peace.'

We crossed the road and entered the leafy park, where I sat Gerard down on a bench and explained the absence of Hogarth and Swift. He took the news quite well, though it obviously came as a shock.

'So I presume,' he said at length, 'that Macaulay will be leaving us in due course too.'

'I'm afraid so,' I replied.

'That's a bit sad.'

'Agreed,' I said, 'but I'm certain he wouldn't want us to be sentimental about it.'

Gerard fell silent as he considered the recent revelations. There was a lot to take in, and several minutes went by before he spoke again.

'This new list,' he said. 'All the episodes from the past that we've come to regret. Rather long, isn't it?'

'Yes,' I said, 'and I doubt if we're anywhere near the end.'

'In which case, it hardly reflects very favourably on England.'

'Well, no,' I conceded, 'taken in isolation it doesn't; but you have to remember we always have a trump card up our sleeve.'

'What's that then?'

'The Mansfield Judgement of 1772.'

'Oh yes?'

'It was a landmark decision actually, when a slave became free merely by setting foot on English soil.'

'That's more like it!' Gerard exclaimed. 'Something honourable and glorious!'

'Quite.'

'Why on earth didn't Macaulay mention it?'

'Perhaps he didn't want to sound boastful,' I suggested. 'Not his way of doing things at all.'

'No, you're probably right,' said Gerard. 'Even so, I wish he wouldn't keep dwelling on that damned list. It can't be doing him any good.'

We rose from the bench and headed homeward. All across the park, the trees were stirring in the breeze; and dark ripples moved swiftly over the ornamental lake. It was supposed to be summer, but autumn was already drawing near.

38.

'England is a naturally peaceful country,' said Macaulay, 'but when our colonies were threatened plainly something needed to be done.'

He was telling us about the colonies in America; and how the settlers became increasingly alarmed at French expansion along the Mississippi River. They felt themselves encircled in the west; furthermore, their trade was restricted, so they approached the crown authorities in search of a remedy.

'The settlers desired a greater say in the way their land was governed, taxed and defended,' continued Macaulay. 'but the British refused to listen and soon these grievances turned to outright rebellion.'

The Wednesday evening talk was well attended. Herbert sat in the front row as usual, making copious notes, while Gerard and I occupied seats at the back, and once again I was impressed by Macaulay's declamatory style.

It was especially interesting to observe the way he distinguished between British belligerence and English peacefulness. Tonight's subject was the American War of Independence, and he went to great lengths to emphasize the fact that, by and large, the English public sympathized with the colonists' plight; and that it was Great Britain's heavy-handedness which caused us to lose our prize possession.

'Nonetheless,' he added, 'the real culprits were the French.'

At this point Herbert raised his hand.

'But surely,' he said, 'the French had as much right to be in America as anybody else.'

'Maybe so,' replied Macaulay, 'but we didn't want the whole world speaking French, did we?'

'Suppose not.'

'And for similar reasons we were obliged to expel all the French colonists from India.'

Privately I debated whether 'we' in this instance meant the English or the British. The distinction, I was coming to realize, was very subtle. Down in the front row I noticed Herbert making further notes, but he said nothing more.

The mention of the French, meanwhile, had reminded me of a separate question which I'd been meaning to ask Macaulay for some time. It wasn't a matter for the general ear, however, so I decided to leave it until after the talk, which was now reaching its natural conclusion.

'It was during this period,' announced Macaulay, 'that the first steam engines tottered into life. Yet their noisy clattering was nothing compared with the violent convulsions taking place overseas. Turmoil shook India, Egypt, the Caribbean, America and Europe. Only in England did the peace remain intact.'

With these closing words he turned and headed for the doorway, pursued by a flurry of disciples. Amongst them was Herbert, and I noticed he no longer wore a tailcoat with shiny buttons up the front.

When Gerard and I got downstairs we found Macaulay sitting in dignified solitude at our usual table. We bought a round of drinks and joined him.

'Quite a challenging few years ahead,' I ventured. 'Napoleon on the march and so forth.'

'Indeed,' said Macaulay. 'I assume you've been reading ahead.'

'Yes.'

'That's good.'

'But I don't suppose we'll be covering the Retreat from Moscow, will we?'

This was the question I'd been meaning to ask Macaulay, but he appeared astonished by my enquiry.

'Whatever gave you that idea?' he demanded.

'Well......because it had nothing to do with England at peace.'

'On the contrary,' he replied. 'It had everything to do with it.'

'Oh.'

'Napoleon's antics had been disrupting our trade for a decade, and recovery began only after he'd failed at Moscow.'

'So trade is paramount, is it?' I asked.

'Absolutely,' said Macaulay. 'All our historical dealings have hinged ultimately around trade.'

'Which depends on peace and then leads to prosperity.'

'Correct.' He gave me a nod of approval. 'You seem to have attained a good grasp of the subject.'

His comment reminded me of a school report I'd received many years before (in History).

39.

'What's all this about a new list?' said Josephine.

It was the following Monday and she was pulling pints for me and Gerard, but she refused to hand them over until I'd answered her question.

'Well, as far as I know,' I said, 'it's a list of episodes in which England doesn't appear in a particularly good light.'

'So Macaulay won't be mentioning them?'

'Probably not.'

'I see.'

'Not to worry though,' I added. 'There are plenty of colourful events coming up.'

'Such as?'

'The Battle of Trafalgar.'

'But that was fought off the coast of Spain,' she countered. 'It had nothing to do with England at peace.'

'On the contrary,' I said. 'It had everything to do with it. We had to protect our trade, which meant keeping command of the sea, so when Nelson won at Trafalgar he effectively restored the peace that led to prosperity.'

I'd learnt from Macaulay that there was an explanation for everything as long as it was properly worded. I was also aware that this first attempt had been slightly jumbled. Nevertheless, Josephine appeared at least partially convinced.

'What about the Battle of Waterloo?' she asked.

'The same,' I replied. 'Finished off Napoleon and left us free to trade with whoever we wanted.'

'The Battle of New Orleans?'

'The last engagement in a trade war with the United States.'

'The Charge of the Light Brigade?'

'An indirect action to help protect our trade with India.'

'So that English people could drink tea in peace,' added Gerard.

Josephine eyed him coolly.

'I wouldn't know about that,' she said. 'I only drink coffee.'

At last she let us have our pints, which I duly paid for.

'Anyway,' I said, 'how did you find out about the list?'

'Herbert told me,' she replied. 'He worked it out through a process of logical induction.'

'Oh yes?'

'He also informed me that Macaulay would be bowing out very shortly. He said it was something to do with the 'constraints of time'.'

'Yes, well, he's probably correct.'

'Never mind,' she said. 'You can take over.'

'Me?' I said, with surprise. 'But I only know bits and pieces: hardly enough for an entire talk.'

'Can't be helped,' she answered. 'You'll just have to read ahead, won't you?'

40.

On Wednesday morning, Gerard and I went to see Macaulay, only to find his room locked. We knocked and waited, but there was no response, so we decided to see if he'd gone for a stroll in the park. Deep down, however, we both suspected we'd seen the last of him; and after a fruitless search we gave up.

'That's a bit sad,' said Gerard.

'Agreed,' I said, 'but 'I'm certain he wouldn't want us to be sentimental about it.'

During the afternoon, with Josephine's permission, we painted an inscription on the walls of the function room. When we'd finished it read:

CONSIDER HISTORY, WITH THE BEGINNINGS OF IT STRETCHING DIMLY INTO THE REMOTE TIME, EMERGING DARKLY OUT OF THE MYSTERIOUS ETERNITY: THE TRUE EPIC POEM AND DIVINE UNIVERSAL SCRIPTURE.

I then went home and read every history book I could lay my hands on. In the meantime, Gerard prepared a new poster for the noticeboard announcing '**ENGLAND AT PEACE**'.

Around seven-fifteen we sat at our usual table watching people begin trooping upstairs. It was a sizeable crowd and I hoped they wouldn't be too disappointed when they discovered Macaulay wasn't delivering the talk.

'Don't worry,' said Gerard. 'Just do your best.'

'Alright, I'll try,' I said, though I had to admit I was a little apprehensive.

At seven-thirty we headed up to the function room. Gerard made for his favourite seat at the back while I surveyed my audience.

Which is when I realized somebody had slipped passed us unobserved. Sitting in the front row was Herbert, and beside him sat Douglas, bolt upright with his arms folded and apparently in a combative mood.

'England at peace, is it?' he murmured. 'We'll see about that.'

The Author

Magnus Mills was shortlisted for the Booker Prize in 1998.

Printed in Great Britain
by Amazon